PRAISE FOR VLADIMIR'S MUSTACHE

"Elegant, classic stories that sift through history and paint a luminous portrait of an enduring cast of Russian characters. Clark is marvelously protean here, engaging multiple personalities and points of view, and his cold eye and ready wit shine through brilliantly."

– T. C. Boyle

"All Hail Stephan Clark! With terrific gusto, insight, and compassion, Clark's first book of short stories brilliantly illuminates the lives of men and women trapped in Russian history and the muddled post-Soviet present. *Vladimir's Mustache* is a solid achievement, as well as a beguiling introduction to a new literary talent."

– Ken Kalfus

"*Vladimir's Mustache* is a thrilling discovery: dark, elegant fables that dissect the Russian soul, in a style that feels timeless yet utterly fresh. I read each story with a delicious sense of anticipation and dread. Stephan Clark is a marvelous writer, and a tender chronicler of the doomed."

– Karl Iagnemma

"Stephan Clark's very fine story collection is a tour de force of historical imagination. Clark clearly knows the territory, and he brings it to life with an inventiveness and artistry that few writers can match. These wry, wonderful, often revelatory stories mark the debut of a truly gifted writer, and I look forward to reading more books by Stephan Clark."

– Ben Fountain

"Stephan Clark's fiction is serious and funny at the same time, joke followed by intrigue, intrigue followed by insight, and a reader's dream fulfilled. Go get this book before the knock comes."

– Rusty Barnes, *(... Magazine*

"Stephan Clark's stories span ... Russian history in heartbreaking, bre... ...arvelous collection combines an Old W... ..., giving us characters that resonate as c... ..., yet as familiar as our own friends and neighbors. You will find yourself lost, totally immersed in these stories – an experience you don't want to miss."

– Jodee Stanley, Editor, *Ninth Letter*

VLADIMIR'S MUSTACHE

and other stories

Stephan Eirik Clark

Russian Life
BOOKS

Cover: A photographic file of victims of Stalin's terror, in the archives of Memorial, a group dedicated to preserving the memory of Soviet era repression. © Sergey Maximishin. Used with permission.

ISBN 978-1-880100-71-4
Published February, 2012
Library of Congress Control Number: 2011943360

Russian Information Services, Inc.
PO Box 567
Montpelier, VT 05601-0567
www.russianlife.com
orders@russianlife.com
phone 802-223-4955

To my parents, for their support;
and Nastia, without whom I would not care to believe:
Всё будет хорошо!

CONTENTS

THE LADY WITH THE STRAY DOG

There was no talk when a new one appeared on the street; one stray was no different than the next. You treated them like the missionaries in Shevchenko Park or the Ladas racing by at unconscionable speeds: you looked only long enough to step out of the way. The lady reacted no differently. As she emerged from Sovietskaya Station, she saw a short-legged stray approaching and instinctively hurried away from it, her low heels quickly carrying her around the massive thermometer that rose five stories up the side of the former House of Labor, inside of which you could now buy pirated DVDs and imported women's underwear.

Only after Olya had passed the Internet café did she realize the black and gold mutt was still trotting along at her side, its tongue lolling out and its head hanging low to the ground. The thing looked like a German Shepherd that had been reduced to an absurd size by some irreversible blast of science. Olya cursed it softly and offered it a timid kick without breaking stride, then quickened her pace and turned the corner toward the bank, where she processed loans in the small business department.

She thought nothing more of the dog until the following Saturday, when on a walk through Victory Park she stopped at a bench near the fountain and opened a book of classic stories. As she sat there pretending to read, several wedding parties jostled for position not far from her, each waiting to have their picture taken beneath the grand white archway that overlooked the reflecting pond. Olya liked to look at the dresses. Every minute or two, she'd glance up from her book to inspect the latest bride and arrive at a silent judgment. *Too fat for that. Or is she already pregnant?* While doing this near midday, when the sun hanging overhead left her without even the company of a shadow, she noticed the dog sitting at her feet, smiling hideously and panting.

Olya thought to concentrate on her story. It was a tale of love and passion misdirected by confusion and deceit, one she'd read more than a few times before. But she couldn't do it. The couple at the far end of the bench – they had sat down after her – laughed to themselves and made a comment about the dog. Olya offered the girl a fixed, sidelong look. She was no more than sixteen but already sitting in her boyfriend's lap and sharing his cigarette and beer when she wasn't kissing him on the mouth. The girl whispered something into her boyfriend's ear and laughed again, and this infuriated Olya. She had sat on the bench first; they had come after she was already there. But now she was unable to read or look at the dresses in peace. She closed her book and marched off, getting a handful of paces away before turning to stamp her foot at the dog.

It couldn't be scared. It followed her down the tree-shaded path toward the curb, where two wedding witnesses stood smoking by a white Mercedes wrapped in colorful blue and gold ribbons and decorated with flowers. It even crossed the street at her side and followed her down Sumskaya Street, all the way to the steps that descended into Sovietskaya Station. Here, Olya turned to question it with a strained look.

"What?" she said. "What?!"

The dog barked. Behind it a crowd of young men and women stood beneath the thermometer on the side of the former House of Labor, a popular place to meet in Kharkov. Everyone was looking around expectantly or tapping away at the buttons of their mobile phones. The dog continued to look at Olya with no less urgency or expectation, then barked a second and a third time.

She cursed it once more and rushed down past the line of kiosks into the depths of the station, not looking back until she was past the swinging doors and onto the escalator. As she dropped toward the tracks, confident now that she was alone, she remembered the young girl on the park bench. Stupid where I'm smart, she thought. She stepped onto the platform, then, conceding the rest while looking into the dark tunnel for the train. And playful where I'm serious.

The following Tuesday, with the streets still dark and slick from an early morning rain, the mutt brushed Olya's ankle as she emerged from the metro station. She reached for her umbrella and opened it into the dog's face, but in doing so she backed into the path of a man coming up the steps behind her. She spun around, apologizing and pushing back at her short red hair, but the man only mumbled and hunched his shoulders into the chill of the air as he skirted around her and headed down toward the river.

When she got to the bank, Olya fixed herself a cup of tea in the common room, then returned to the office that held her cubicle and two others.

"He followed me again today," she told Dmitri. "The same one."

Dmitri pushed his chair back from his computer and turned to offer a frown in Olya's direction. "Maybe no one feeds him," he said. "Have you considered that? You should show some mercy."

They had been flirting ever since she'd left her job at the department store and taken up loan processing – flirting, she reminded herself, despite the framed family portraits that crowded in around his computer.

"Mercy?" she said. "Because he can't find scraps to eat himself?"

"Can't find? Aren't there." He stood now with one arm draped over the partition between their cubicles. "Things aren't as they were when we were children. This used to be a good Russian street."

A voice from the far cubicle called out to him, "You live in Ukraine, Dmitri."

This was Anton Ivanovich Shumenko, a man who wielded his Ukrainian surname like a stick. Dmitri ignored him. His people were from Kursk, just across the border, and like many ethnic Russians living here, he acted as if Ukraine were a dream only believed in the West.

"Times were gentler then," he said. "A nice woman would always open her window and toss out some meaty scraps. But now half the apartments in the city center are empty, or they've been refurbished and rented out to German and American sex tourists."

Olya grinned over her tea-cup. "Dieses ist fantastisch! Ooh-la-la!"

Dmitri shook his head with a politician's practiced show of disapproval. His mother worked for the gas company. She checked the meters inside the apartments on Bazhanova Street, where the previous month a German in mesh bikini underwear had answered her knock with his TV still playing foreign pornography from the room down the hall. *Ooh-la-la! Dieses ist fantastisch!*

"This is what they expect," Dmitri said. "To open their doors and have prostitutes walk in. They're no better than the Germans in the war. Sixty years ago, they filled their railroad cars with black earth and shipped it home. Now it's our women they're after."

"When did he realize your mother wasn't the prostitute?"

Dmitri turned to the other cubicle. "Don't tempt me, Anton," he said, before falling back into his chair and continuing to Olya, "You should feed that dog. It's a good Russian dog. You think the Germans care if it lives or dies?"

Olya had turned on her computer and was waiting for her home page to load. When it finally did, she saw she had three personal e-mails in her inbox. Two were from colleagues in the small business department; one was from a single woman a few years older than her who had bought a second apartment after being transferred into the division that granted corporate loans. All of the messages had been forwarded. And they made her laugh, the best of them at least, but she wished she could come in one morning and expect to receive something else.

That night, a disembodied voice turned her round from her computer screen and sent her gaze out the door to the giant crystal chandelier that dropped five stories from the ceiling of the uppermost floor to the lobby. It was the type of decoration Olya had once thought deserving of a Tolstoy novel. When she'd first walked up the staircase encircling it, the chandelier had made her imagine a great ball and a princess and white silk gloves worn to the elbow. But now that she'd worked at the bank for more than a year, the chandelier was somehow invisible, something she turned to with unfocused green eyes whenever the time was announced on the company's hidden speaker system.

"Dear Workers," the recording began, "it is now 9:45 and the bank will be closing its doors in fifteen minutes."

Olya picked up her things before the recording could finish and was moving across the landing to the stairs, still pushing her arms into her coat, when the company anthem, debuted only the previous month, began to play.

"I can understand making us listen to this in the morning," she said to Dmitri as he hurried down the stairs in front of her. "But why at night? Am I supposed to go home and dream of the bank?"

"Each time I hear it," he said, "I feel as if Brezhnev is pinning a medal on my chest."

"Then my fears are right. This is a period of stagnation."

Dmitri said nothing further before reaching the lobby. He was busy with his mobile phone, quickly tapping out a message to his wife. Olya stopped beneath the giant chandelier and watched him move away from her, past the three seated security guards and through the glass door. When he was gone, she realized the guards were looking at her with unblinking eyes. Her own phone buzzed in her purse. It was an SMS from Lena, who was waiting with the others at the café Gogol-Mogol. Olya began tapping out her reply as she started for the door and was answered outside by a bark.

The dog was up the street from her, on the corner facing the door to the grocery store. It barked so loudly that it bounced on its front legs. It could see someone coming from inside, a man in blue jeans and a pair of white sneakers – an American, obviously. Who else would think he could walk the streets and stay clean?

The man held a tube of bologna, which he unwrapped while crouching down before the dog. Olya walked as quickly as she could, not returning his look when she circled out into the street to pass around them.

She entered the café speaking of the dog. While hanging her jacket at the stand and pulling up a red chair beside the birthday girl, she spoke of the animal as if it were possessed: "What else is he doing if not haunting me? I see him every day."

Lena poured her a glass of sweet Georgian wine. Olya took it and pulled a package of L'Oreal mascara from her purse.

"It's not much," she said to Lena, "but at least you know it's real." She explained the rest to the other four girls – all of them twenty-seven or twenty-eight – gathered around the two small tables they'd pulled together: "One of my clients bought it on a trip to Munich. It's Duty Free."

They nodded to show their approval, all except Vika, who sat smoking silently on the padded red bench against the wall. Since the group's last birthday celebration, she'd gained four or five kilos, leaving her eyes sunk down into the flesh of her face like cherries in a cup of softened ice cream. "But you didn't tell us," she said, "is he at least good looking?"

"Who?"

"The dog."

"Oh!" Olya swallowed awkwardly – they'd ordered pizza – and reached for her wine. "What do I know? He's a dirty little beast. Small enough to kick, but so mean you wouldn't dare. Only the Devil knows what breed."

She laughed, then almost shrieked as she pointed up to the line of windows that looked out onto the sidewalk. It was the dog again, running alongside the foreigner in the white sneakers.

"I'm caught in a Chekhov story! He's going to follow me home one night to bed!"

Vika stamped out her cigarette. "If only I were so lucky. Olya, Lena – everyone has someone but me."

Laughter rose up all around their tables, loud enough to make the other patrons look. Olya turned to Lena, not understanding what the others already knew.

"I'm getting married," Lena explained. "That's the big news! Derrick asked me last night. He'll submit the paperwork next week."

Olya tried to remember which one it could be. The Norwegian or the American? Derrick. Two had visited that summer, one right after the other, neither sufficiently rich nor attractive enough to differentiate himself in Olya's mind. She hoped it was the latter. She couldn't imagine her friend's children speaking a language of some four or five million – you couldn't go from Russian to that.

Olya shook her head. "So how long until…?"

"Who knows," Lena said. "Months maybe. I'll know more after the embassy calls me in for the interview."

"And the chest X-ray," said Vika, lighting a new cigarette. "Why did I major in economics? I could've opened a shop selling chest X-rays to all the women leaving town. I could've become so rich I wouldn't care that I'm alone."

"What happened to Zhenya?"

"She's not alone."

Vika set down her lighter. "Not even when I'm with Zhenya."

"Give me a few months," Lena told her. "I'll find you an American."

Vika waved away the suggestion. "Why are all these American men single? What happened to the American women? Was there a plague?"

"There was a McDonald's!"

The girls laughed again, and Olya was glad for it. Their good humor allowed her to hide in her thoughts. She'd never believed her friend would actually go through with it. For three years Lena had dated foreigners she'd met online: Americans, a Canadian, an Australian and a few Brits, and then that lumbering Norwegian who'd spoken of buying investment property in Kharkov. Olya had always believed that dating foreigners was something Lena did for excitement, so she could go to nice restaurants or nightclubs she otherwise couldn't afford. But Olya hadn't thought Lena would take it any further than receiving a few gifts. She thought it was about simple fun, about waking up and finding more than a few funny pictures in your e-mail.

"Derrick?" Olya said. "He's the American?"

Lena nodded. "Michigan," she said. *Mitch-e-gun.* "He says it snows like here."

When Olya returned to her apartment, she found the light on in the kitchen and her mother at the stove in a long striped nightshirt and brown slippers. Olya said a quiet hello, received one just as quiet in return, and went to the fridge for a cup of kefir. After a few minutes, they heard her younger brother, Vova, down the hall. Or rather, they heard his new girlfriend, a student at the police academy. Vova had been just a year or two old when the Berlin Wall came down. Olya and her brother were from different generations, even if they were only separated by six or seven years. Beautiful little animals, Olya thought. The girlfriend screamed loudly enough for all of them to hear.

The second or third time it happened, Olya had wondered why her mother didn't confront Vova. But now she understood. Her mother didn't want to lose him. She and Olya's father slept in the living room so their children could each have a room of their own. They were separated from the slaps and screams that started each night after nine or ten by only a thin wall. But Olya's mother couldn't say anything. If she did, it would only send him away from her, possibly for good. And so even when you're married, Olya thought, you still worry that you might die alone. It depressed her more than anything she could remember. It had been four years since Sasha.

"Lena's getting married," she said, just so she and her mother could distract themselves with conversation. "To an American. He lives in Michigan."

Olya's mother nodded, skimming the fat from the surface of her broth. "Marriage is good for a young woman."

Olya drank her kefir in steady, vaguely medicinal gulps. It made her sad to think her mother did not say anything more forceful, that she was no longer as she had been when Olya was still at the university. "When are you going to find another boyfriend?" her mother had asked. "What are you going to do when you're through with your studies and there's no work and no men?" There had been a kind of hopefulness about her then, when she still felt confident enough to raise her voice.

Olya's brother came out in his underwear and went to the bathroom for a pair of nail clippers.

"Vova," Olya's mother said. "Kefir?"

"No, mama. Nothing."

Olya sighed as he turned back to his room. The kitchen smelled of boiled chicken. She took another sip of kefir, thinking of the dog again, and then of Dmitri, and then of the two of them together. She wasn't about to feed it, not in the street like that foreign man, and she wouldn't dare bring it home, even if her father would allow it. One couldn't live that way. Sure, she could clean its matted fur and brush its yellow teeth, but it'd still jump up to take food from the table and wake her at six, pushing its wet nose into her side, or barking to ask for a walk. It'd be nice to have someone there when she walked in each night; she wanted to feel a kiss on her cheek. But then she'd walk through the apartment and find its fur all over the place, its smell everywhere, and maybe a little turd behind the sofa or a bold one right there in the middle of the rug. She couldn't do it. And besides, Dmitri was already married.

Olya took her cup to the sink. "Vika's gained weight," she said.

Her mother nodded at the stove, saying she'd spoken to Vika's mother. "Is she still with that married man?"

Olya shrugged. What was there to say? Silence and the convenience of Vika's neighborhood – close to his work, far from his apartment – were the keys to their relationship. "Just don't let me see you with anyone else," Vika had told him.

"She'll always be stealing other women's men," Olya said, surprising even herself. "That's all she knows."

Her mother pulled the spoon out of the soup and set it down beside the pot. "Have you seen Sasha?"

"Mom." It was all she needed to say. It was over. He was three girls on from her at least. They said their goodnights then, and soon Olya was lying alone in her narrow bed, a bed she'd slept in for so long that her body had formed in it a deep valley. Shortly after midnight, her brother and his girlfriend started up again. Olya counted the number of times his girlfriend screamed.

★

For the next two nights, Olya worked late, giving her time to several accounts in various stages of completion, including one she wanted to see succeed more than the rest. It was a request for a loan of 170,000 grivna from a man she'd known at the university. He needed the money to purchase a new Freightliner truck and increase the trade he did between Russia and Ukraine. Despite the profitability of these transactions, Olya wasn't confident.

"I understand you'll pay the money back," she told him from the café on her phone. "But you have to understand – your business shows a complete lack of accountability, even by today's standards. Everyone's keeping two sets of books, and you don't even have one."

"I have two Freightliner trucks. American," he said. "They're not even three years old. If the bank doesn't get its money, they can come for them." Olya started to explain that this wasn't what they wanted, but he spoke over her, saying it wasn't attractive for a woman to argue. "Just try. You watch. I'll get my money, and then I'll take you out and we'll celebrate. Agreed?"

Olya left the café thinking back on their time together at the university, when he'd flirted with her and she'd only held back because she'd had her eye on Sasha. Just then, the dog barked, and Olya came to a stop on the sidewalk, clutching at the collar of her white coat. The creature stood outside the door to the market, so excited that it ran in small circles between its barks. The foreigner came out with another chunk of bologna and bent over to feed the dog from his hand.

Olya smiled and caught his eye as she passed, but as she continued around the corner toward the metro she told herself that this wasn't enough – she should have stopped, struck up a conversation, asked if he was American. "I have a friend marrying a man from Michigan," she could have said. Isn't that how it worked? She stopped outside the Internet café and turned around to look in his direction. She could still go back. She could pass him again and this time say a few words. But this was crazy – she turned and continued into the metro station, paid for her token, and rode the escalator down. He'd think no better of her following him than she had of the dog. What kind of girl was she?

She realized her mistake only after stepping onto the train and taking a seat. A man doesn't shy away from a woman who follows him home; he looks forward to the day. The door closed. The train pulled away. She rode home listening to an old man sing an old Soviet song as he walked the length of the car, shaking a plastic cup with Stalin's face on it.

The next morning, Olya left the meeting of the credit committee in the sixth-floor conference room with the result she'd anticipated all week: a rejected application for her friend's new truck.

She should have denied the loan herself. No one else in her department would have allowed it to go this far. Everyone knew Vitaly lived in a village near the border and met each week with three men who drove vans bearing the numbers 77 or 99 on their license plates. Moscow. It was a simple exchange: poultry from Kiev for frozen fish from Murmansk. And though the business was good, it wasn't the thing for a bank. Stupid, she told herself. It had been stupid to even try.

"They didn't give me the money?" he said when she called to share the news.

Vitaly argued like so many men, she thought. Not with new arguments, not with facts, only with louder echoes of what he'd already said.

"The bank is not a pawn shop, Vitaly. We earn money on interest, not by selling used trucks."

"Did you talk like this to the credit committee?"

Olya didn't answer. She wanted to hear what she was afraid she already knew.

"Why don't you ever try saying something sweet? You're a woman. You should talk like one."

She hung up after telling him to come back to her when he could show her the receipts.

That afternoon, Olya followed Dmitri into the company cafeteria on the second floor, nodding along to his talk of a recent family trip to St. Petersburg.

"If I were Putin," he said, "I'd keep the foreigner fee what it is," – three times the Russian price of admission to state museums – "but why stop there? If the Germans want to visit the same museums they once bombed, why should they pay the same as the Bulgarians? Or the Americans even? And if the Japanese at the Peterhof ask me one more time to step out of the frame, why shouldn't they pay ten times the normal price? Didn't we win the war?"

Olya abandoned her tray in front of the soup tureens and apologized to Dmitri, saying she needed to visit the pharmacy. It was a remark so vague, she knew he would imagine the feminine and dare not question her. As for the purpose of her deceit, Olya didn't know it herself until she was on her way out through the lobby. She didn't want to talk politics with Dmitri anymore. That was all they ever did, and she couldn't bear it any longer. She'd read so many books, knew so many stories, but suddenly this was no longer enough. It hurt her to admit the truth to herself in plain direct words: Olya wanted to fall in love.

She walked to the corner store and waited at the counter for the saleswoman to say she was listening. Olya ordered some cold *vareniki* and a bottle of Narzan, and while paying asked about the American.

"He must be American," Olya said. "He wears white tennis shoes in this weather. They have no conception of dirt."

"Oh!" The woman smiled, showing her gold teeth as she dug into the front pocket of her blue smock for Olya's change. "He buys boiled sausage, the same now for three days."

"For the dog," Olya said.

The woman shrugged as if a man's motives were of no interest to her. "Every day before closing, that's all I know." She lifted her chin then, looking to the woman behind Olya. "I'm listening!"

Olya left the store, thinking she'd get off early that night and sit for a time in front of the opera house. He would probably be in Kharkov for only a few more days, fewer if he were visiting as part of a three- or four-city romance tour. He might be dating someone already, a woman with whom he'd shared a lengthy correspondence online or a handful of brief telephone calls. Or perhaps he wasn't a bride hunter at all. He could be an academic sent here to teach or to advise some project, an American scholar escaping the familiar and mundane by researching the post-Soviet.

She walked up the steps of the massive concrete opera house, passing young boys and girls kissing or linking arms, and sat on a bench facing the street. She set her bag of *vareniki* in her lap and drank from her bottle of mineral water, telling herself this foreign man was a creature of habit, no different from her. She only needed to come back and wait for him to appear, because they were joined together in a trinity: the woman, the man, the dog.

No sooner had Olya thought this than she heard the noise – a screeching of tires, one horn answering another, then the sharp crash of metal. She looked up after hearing a bark – more of a yelp, really – and saw two steaming Ladas nose-to-nose in the street.

She stood up and moved into the gathering crowd. Two men had gotten out of their cars and were now squared off over their bellies, each pointing at the other's dirt-covered Lada and screaming obscenities. Olya pushed through to the front as if expecting to find a family member on the ground, when instead it was of course only the dog, her dog.

Two deaf teenagers stood closest to it, speaking to each other in sign. The dog lay on its side in the gutter, panting, with its legs stretched lame behind it, as if it had been struck in the midst of a great leap.

Olya looked around, smelling benzene and seeing people's breath cloud the air. Her mind had been trained to analyze risks and rewards. She was tired and hungry and she sank down beside the dog, collapsing onto one side and sitting on the meaty flesh of her leg. The deaf students traded signs more urgently, biting into their lower lips. Two older women with covered hair bent down toward her and spoke loudly, but Olya barely heard them. She knew only that the American couldn't know. If he went for a walk in the middle of the day and saw the dog lying there, dead, he'd have no reason to return in the evening, when Olya could expect to see him.

She picked up the dog, rising under its weight with a wobble.

"She's mad!" an old woman said, reaching for Olya's elbow. "Put that thing down!"

"The diseases!" said another.

But Olya shook the woman's hand away and ran through a break in traffic to the park on the other side of the street. The dog's eyes were watery and black, fluid as an oil slick. She sat on a bench to catch her breath and stroked the dog's matted gray fur, pleased to see it react to her touch with a few loose movements of its tongue. She cooed, and it answered in a soft voice, its language lost in a gurgle of blood at the back of its throat. Then the animal's breathing slowed and the blacks of its eyes grew shallower, and Olya, cradling the dog more tightly in her arms, rose from the bench, not seeing the crowd around her, only looking for a way to escape.

YAGODA'S BULLETS

Before his arrest and execution, Genrikh Yagoda, the leader of the Soviet secret police, was an avid collector of historical memorabilia. Whenever one of the more famous old revolutionaries fell from Stalin's favor (and consequently required the attention of a pistol's puff of smoke) Yagoda would ask that the historic bullet be extricated from either bone or flesh and transferred to a candy dish he kept on his desk. From there, the bullet would be moved to a glass display case that hung on the wall, in which each of Yagoda's snub-nosed mementos were arranged in the fashion of a prized collection of butterflies. "This one," he would say, "is Zinoviev. Here, Kamenev. And the green felt against which they are pinned? Torn from a snooker table belonging to Tsar Nikolai II himself."

Many times, owing to the relative independence of his position, Yagoda could personally fire the pistol, extract the bullet, and place the specimen within its frame himself. Once, however, when he was shot and killed by his successor, such pleasures were not his own. Following Yagoda's death, his bullets remained with his executioner, Nikolai Yezhov, who in turn was shot and killed by his successor, Lavrenti Beria. Beria did not possess the poetic sensibilities of his predecessors. He ordered the bullets transferred to the State Archive of the October Revolution, where they were filed alongside an inventory of Yezhov's life: "revolver bullets, blunted, wrapped in paper, inscribed Zinoviev, Kamenev, Yagoda . . ."

This took place when black cars moved through the streets late at night, stopping only to deliver one's terror. Anything could result in your arrest: a careless word at a café, the wrong acquaintance in your youth. No one was safe, not even Stalin's father, who had been reduced to begging after abandoning his family so many years before. Rumor had it he disappeared after bellowing drunk once too often, "You refuse me? You refuse to give money to me? I made Stalin! With these hips, I made The Man of Steel!"

They were uncertain times, that is for certain. And so when not informing on informers, people praised Stalin in their diaries, if only so their testimony might later be introduced in court and used in their defense. But then the purge expanded with all the logic of a lottery and fear became its only goal. People no longer answered the door. At a certain hour it could mean but one thing, and there was no escape. You would be hauled away, presented with the confession required of you, and sent off to some camp, if not against the wall.

So hearing the thump of a foot thrown into the front door or the groan of a hinge straining beneath the weight of a pressed shoulder, people stood unmoving in the kitchen until at last they knew they needed to act. One year, jumping was at the height of fashion. People threw themselves from the windows of offices and communal apartment buildings, often shouting party slogans as they fell: "Land, peace and bread!" "All power to the soviets!" Even those souls assigned to live on the ground floor were not necessarily denied, for if they saw a black car appear outside their window, they could race up the stairs to a window of a more desirable height and wait to see whose number had been called and if they should resign themselves to gravity.

If this was in fact the case, they would not be the only victim, for a person walking by below would no less be the inheritor of a great misfortune. After all, when he heard the body land – with a rude splatter in summer or a polite and muffled thud into the snows of winter – he would need the presence of mind not to call out to God in either prayer or recrimination, for He too had been vanquished alongside the tsar.

KAMKOV THE ASTRONOMER

One night at his dacha, Stalin looked up from his meal of bread, sausage, and smoked carp to consider a matter of celestial importance. With him in the study were Comrades Kaganovich and Molotov, who stood at the far window arguing about a constellation. The one said it was Cassiopeia, the other Orion. Stalin wiped the crumbs from his mustache, eager for the debate. Such matters had fascinated him since his youth in the seminary, when he'd often tilted back on his heels to puzzle over the stars. He never had been able to make sense of the heavens. Where others saw bears and scorpions and chained ladies, he saw only a messy splatter of light.

Molotov returned to the low table around which they had gathered, while Kaganovich circled the room, defending his position at great length and with great volume. He provided Molotov with Cassiopeia's mythological origins, and drew meaning between each of the bright dots in the sky. He gestured. He laughed at perceived errors in logic. And he even touched on phrenology, a philosophy he refused to endorse in the end, but one he still found worthy of mention, considering Molotov's limited grasp of the sciences and the flat spot on the back of his head. Stalin was impressed. He grunted and gave short nods of approval. But Molotov could not be so easily swayed, just as he could not be bothered to fortify his defense. "It is

Orion," he said, simply and completely, before smiling as if only a fool would believe otherwise.

Kaganovich lunged at Molotov's throat, causing Stalin to shake with laughter and Molotov to rise fighting to his feet. The two men scuffled. The one pushed at the other and the other pushed back, and then they were knocking into the table and shaking the many pieces of china and silver that had been placed there. Stalin's tea cup jumped, splashing its contents across a pile of papers. This ended the argument. It turned Stalin's laughter into a bark and caused Kaganovich to release the foreign minister's throat.

Stalin snatched his papers from the table. The top one had received a messy brown splatter, but the names were still legible, the list still intact. He frowned, grimly satisfied, and pressed the top sheet into the chest of his high-collared green tunic, absorbing what had been spilled. "The matter can be very easily settled," he said. "We will call the astronomers. The astronomers will decide this."

It was not unusual for the Moscow Planetarium to be staffed at such a late hour. Stalin's day was the world's night, and so his schedule was kept by all the leaders of all the institutions, who feared nothing more than a phone left ringing in the dark. What was unusual, at least in the Soviet Union's brief history, was for the planetarium's director to not be an astronomer. Molotov held the receiver steady when he learned this, then covered the mouthpiece to announce the news. "It seems that several astronomers were disgraced last year in Leningrad, and that as a result certain precautionary measures were ordered to ensure that the Trotskyists could not infiltrate the other observatories and planetariums."

Kaganovich sat forward in his chair, as if expecting to hear himself implicated at the end of all of this.

"Consequently," Molotov concluded, "the director of the Moscow Planetarium is now an officer of the People's Commissariat for Internal Affairs."

Kaganovich released a soft breath, then reset his face into a frown. "And he knows nothing of the stars?"

"Nor the planets," Molotov answered.

Stalin nodded, as if he had expected this all along. But the truth was, he did not remember the disgrace of the astronomers in Leningrad, though he knew he had undoubtedly ordered it. Too many names on too many lists – this was the problem. He signed them in his office over his first cup of tea and added his approval before turning out the lamp in bed. Sometimes Lavrenti Beria, the leader of the secret police, even risked landing on a list himself by knocking on the door of the wash closet. "I would not interrupt," he'd say, "but party member A was seen in City B of Oblast C doing X with the anti-Soviet Y. You'll see I've added their names to the bottom of the list."

Stalin lifted his chin to Molotov. "Disgraced," he said, "yes, of course. But irregardless of the irregularities in Leningrad, surely there remain astronomers in Moscow."

Molotov spoke briefly into the phone to confirm just this, then returned to his chair smiling. "The director has promised to wake the nearest one. We should expect his arrival shortly."

Kaganovich eyed Molotov suspiciously. "It is Cassiopeia," he said.

Molotov poured himself a fresh cup of tea. "Orion."

The previous spring, astronomers from Kiev to Vladivostok had hesitated before their telescopes, as if fearing that upon leaning into the eyepiece they might discover someone at the other end staring back. But then word spreads fast in any professional community and so it was after the purge of the Pulkovo Observatory in Leningrad. No one knew what to believe, only what to say: that the astronomers had been awoken with a knock and dragged off to the Dmitrov jail, where they were charged with being Old Leninists or Trotskyist agents, the definition of which (some privately snickered) many of the accused no doubt required.

Among the unfortunates was the young astronomer Maxim Kamkov, who was considered something of a prodigy by those of his colleagues already assured of their own legacy. Before his arrest, Kamkov had dedicated himself to the field of lunar volcanics, in part because he had sought something higher than what he'd seen as a child, when the revolution had painted everything with blood, and in part because he was so shy he could find no comfort elsewhere. More than once he had promised himself he'd approach Svetlana Borshchagovskaya, the geologist famous for having declared that there is no private property, not even a comrade's genitalia. But each time he looked at her, he found himself unable to talk. And so he worked late each day, and went home each night to the small apartment he shared with a dog so small it considered the apartment large. Until, that is, he was taken to the Dmitrov jail.

Kamkov was one of thirty-three dissidents detained in a single cell. He sat in the middle of the floor with his eyes lifted to the single bulb that hung glowing from a wire above. The light made a noise like a fly trapped in a glass, flickered off and on, and then went black. Kamkov was relieved. He had been here at least thirty-six hours, enough to have slept and awoken and heard that sleep was allowed only five hours each night. The whole time this false sun had shined.

Kamkov looked away from it, then stood and moved toward the far wall. He lifted his chin, as if to a window that had suddenly appeared. "The moon was likely spit out from the earth," he said. "To study it is to study ourselves."

It was June and it was hot and no one answered in the dark. The prisoners were either tossing through feverish dreams or lying down in a vain attempt to suck in a breath of cool air through the cracks in the wooden floorboards.

Kamkov lifted his hand to the window, reaching for what he saw. "It is probably without an atmosphere of its own and deader than even the most barren desert."

"Stop your talking!" This came from a man who knelt at the door with his face pressed into the keyhole, where he'd been waiting for a guard to walk by and generate a breeze. "I'm suffocating enough without your hot air."

Kamkov's hand fell from his window. Could he die in here? And if so, what would happen to his Kashtanka? He saw the dog now as he always had in his mind: a little brown ball of fur with a pink ribbon in its hair, tilting its head to one side as if to question you. Each day, the Yorkshire terrier ran circles in front of the door when it heard Kamkov's approach – for it could tell when he was coming and not one of their neighbors. So smart, Kamkov thought. And yet now she probably sat whimpering, watching the door knob and wondering why it would not turn. Kamkov liked to believe a neighbor would hear the dog's cries, that the superintendent would be called and the dog saved with food and water. But he also remembered the night they had come for the man down the hall, when no one had opened their door despite the screams. By morning it was as if the man hadn't existed. People walked in and out of his apartment, always leaving with more than they had brought. A tea kettle. A pair of shoes. An overcoat. Kamkov wanted to call out to him, to ask him for his forgiveness, but he could not remember the man's name.

The door to the cell swung open, and a guard stepped in kicking the man at the keyhole to one side. "Kamkov!" he yelled, for it was his turn. "Come!"

In the interrogation room, Kamkov was thrown onto the concrete floor, where the coolness of what met him was pleasing until he noticed the box. It sat in front of him, no larger than a cubic meter in size. Beyond it was a desk, behind which sat two agents from the People's Commissariat for Internal Affairs. The first, short and fat, stared at Kamkov. The second, tall and thin, picked at his nails. Kamkov looked again to the box, wondering if small dogs starved more quickly than large ones. They needed less food, he knew, but perhaps what little food they did require was required more urgently so.

"We have learned you are a Trotskyist," the first agent said, to which Kamkov looked up wanting to ask, "Which one was he again?" because quite frankly, Kamkov was not the greatest of revolutionaries.

The second agent reached for a scientific journal that was familiar to the prisoner's eyes. "Your last published paper," he said, "it carries codes for anti-Soviet activity."

Kamkov squinted, wondering for a moment if this were true. But then he remembered that he was the author and it was false. He thought to ask, "What does the code say?"

The second agent looked to the first, and together the two studied the journal, whispering between it and each other. Kamkov's hopes rose. Perhaps it is someone else they are after, he thought. And like that three names came to mind, the names of scientists so sloppy their reputations could only be salvaged if their papers were meant to carry codes and not scientific thoughts. Finally, the second agent stood, admitting that the full extent of the code had not yet been revealed.

"But this does not mean," the first agent said, coming out from behind his desk, "that you should not confess."

"Yes," the second agent agreed, "tell us what you know."

Kamkov made a face that suggested he'd expected coffee and tasted tea. He had no time for more rejoinders. The agents stopped before him, and then the first lifted the box over Kamkov's head. "Confess," he said, and now Kamkov was like a turtle, with his head falling down between his shoulders. "May I have an attorney?" he asked. But no, the box came down on top of him, a box that had nails hammered into it on all sides. Kamkov felt them tear at his skin as the box was pushed in stages to the floor. He screamed and threw his voice into the dark.

"Speak!" one agent said, slapping the box. "Confess and you can go!"

So Kamkov said, "The surface of the moon is pockmarked like the cheeks of Joseph Vissarionovich Stalin!" He thought he had only thought this, but when his box was kicked, and the agent said something of his wit, Kamkov doubted the powers of his restraint.

"Confess!"

But not having committed a crime, unless it was a crime to daydream of the stars, he could only think to say: "I would like to see the other side of the moon! It might greatly influence my theories!"

For which his box received another kick and his wit another curse.

"Confess!"

And yet not having followed the show trials in the papers, he did not even know what lies to say.

"Confess!"

So he screamed, as the nails pushed in against his face, "I fear the other side of the moon will be no different than this!"

"What?"

"That it will be no different than what we can already see!"

Nothing happened. It was dark. Kamkov breathed heavily, hearing beneath this the barking of his dog. Then the box was lifted, again in stages marked by his screams, and set down to offer the first agent a seat. Kamkov sat on the floor panting and bloody, hoping these men had realized their mistake. Then the second agent kicked him in the chest, sending Kamkov's skull back into the concrete until everything in his world went black.

★

The interrogators worked in shifts, going home to their wives and their dogs and their sons and their daughters, while the prisoners were kept without sleep and beaten and humiliated and asked to confess to crimes they did not commit nor often understand. When Kamkov was awakened a fourth, fifth or sixth time – he could not say – one of his first interrogators had returned (the thin one) and with him he had brought a piece of paper and a pencil no larger than a child's thumb.

"Is this what I have done?" Kamkov asked, staring at the paper.

The agent took it from him and turned it right side up. "You sign," he instructed.

So Kamkov did, feeling a rush of love for this man whose pity had released him. Only later, as he was loaded into the cattle car, did he wish he had read what he'd been given and learned what he had not done. For there were six years ahead of him in the gulags, six years that would surely pass with the repetition of the most basic form of small talk. *What did you not do?* He heard the question now, sitting in the cattle car and staring up at its only window, a tiny opening near the top of the compartment that was cross-hatched by barbed-wire. Kamkov could see the moon through it, and from its light the others could see his face, bloodied and broken by the abuse of the nails. *What did you not do?* People asked him this now, but he could not answer because he did not wish to say what he did not know, and he refused to speak anything but the truth. For a man of science this was important. Lies were a future generation's mysteries, after all, and it was from mystery that religion had been born.

Kamkov awoke to a moving train. The sun slanted through the slats in the car, revealing a hole in the middle of the floor. Several prisoners stood around this, feeding it with a crouch or a widening of the legs. Kamkov went to join them, uneasily, and after several minutes found himself with his pants around his ankles and his eyes half-closed. His kidneys throbbed; it felt as if two hands had punched through his sides and begun squeezing what they found there. He bounced with the train, waiting for his morning's relief, but before it could come his legs buckled and he fell backward into the arms of two men.

Kamkov looked over one shoulder and then the other, into the eyes of one man and then the next. "I did not search out friends in this life," he said, speaking like a little boy again. "I had only a dog. My Kashtanka. So smart."

The first man pulled his head far back from Kamkov's and turned cringing to his friend. "Is this a contagious pox I see on his face?"

"Don't be foolish," said the other. "It is from his torture. It is his own blood."

Kamkov smiled as if he had not heard, still limp in the arms of these men. "I am Kamkov," he said. "The astronomer. You are my friends."

The men nodded while correcting their grips, and then Kamkov was held steady before the hole. "Take your time," the first man said.

"You will not fall," said the other.

"We have you now."

But despite these assurances, a grumbling grew among those waiting still farther away, most loudly from the likes of Georgi Egnatashvili, a massive man with a small literary following in the Georgian capital of Tbilisi.

"I write one ill-conceived piece of iambic tetrameter, mocking Stalin's mustache, and how great is the design of my torture?" Egnatashvili looked around him, soliciting the eyes of his audience. "The Boss even thinks to place this man before me – this idiot-child who looks at what his Creator gave him as if he does not know from which end the urine flows!"

"It is Kamkov!" the first man barked. "Kamkov the astronomer."

"He has almost given his life to the state," added the second. "The least you can do is give him is your patience and respect."

Kamkov looked over his shoulder, as if wanting to add something himself. But he could not; he had no strength. Still, it was no matter. Egnatashvili had never seen such a face – a red splatter, like a constellation drawn in blood. "What did you not do?" he asked. Then again, with a turning of his chin that took in those around him: "What did he not do?"

But no one knew, and so no one answered. Instead, as the cattle car rumbled down the tracks, those around Kamkov, led by the poet from Georgia, stood there like children waiting for the communal lavatory. "It is Kamkov," Egnatashvili explained to those only now learning of the delay, "Kamkov the astronomer."

After being unloaded at the train station, the prisoners marched toward the camp. Kamkov first walked with his arms around the shoulders of the men who had helped him at the hole, and then, when they grew too weak, Egnatashvili picked him up and carried him the rest of the way. Finally, the men stopped at an iron gate and walked in together, passing a fence of barbed-wire and coming to a halt on a dirt courtyard surrounded by stone buildings.

A naked man already stood here at attention, not moving though he had a second skin of mosquitoes. On one side of him was a puddle, on the other a guard. When the man flinched, the guard stepped forward and slammed the butt of his rifle on the man's foot. The man cried out and reached for his throbbing appendage, hopping around and shaking the mosquitoes from him like a layer of dust. But this was against the rules, and so the guard slammed his rifle down on the other foot, reminding the man not to move. On being struck a second time, the prisoner allowed his face to go soft with a kind of joy, as if all along he had wanted only this, for his pain to be equal, for it to match. He swayed a moment, then, and slowly regained his balance. When he had it, the mosquitoes returned, falling around his shoulders like a shawl.

"The rules!" the barracks-warden announced, appearing before the prisoners. "We must all follow the rules."

As he spoke, a mosquito landed on the side of Kamkov's neck, directly beneath his ear. Kamkov tried to blow it away. He blew air out of the corner of his mouth and shot it around the side of his neck. But the mosquito circled out of range, and was soon joined by a second and a third and then a fourth. Kamkov was more popular than most. His skin was still bloody from the box; it had not yet scabbed over, and so the mosquitoes smelled him and swarmed. Kamkov blinked and twitched as the barracks-warden spoke. He wanted to defend his own blood with a demonstrative swat or slap, but he feared this too would be against the rules, so he stood there and did not scratch.

In the barracks, Kamkov's bloodied appearance earned him a spot on the bottom-most bunk, a long stretch of planks reserved for those prisoners too weak to climb any higher. They were packed together so closely that whenever one man wanted to turn and sleep on his other side, the whole line had to turn with him. "Left!" a prisoner would shout, and they would turn that way and lie still until another prisoner had them turn back around.

For an hour that night Kamkov flipped like this, wanting always to scratch at his face. There was no relief. If he scratched at a mosquito bite, a scab would bleed; and if he left the scabs alone, the mosquito bites would drive him mad. He wondered, like Egnatashvili, if they had planned this, but then he remembered that there was no plan – that there was not even a 'they.' He was reminded of this as a prisoner above him began to pray:

"In this ever-renewing hell of suffering, in my starvation and agony – "

"Excuse me."

" – and my anxieties and doubts, I ask you Father – "

"Psst!"

" – for your grace and your blessing – "

"I'm talking to you!"

" – so that you may take away my difficulties and show others the glory of your will."

"I said I'm talking to you!" Kamkov kicked at the planks above. "Can you stop that?" The prisoner dropped his face over the end of his bunk. He had whiskers on his chin but none on his skull. "How can you talk to God," Kamkov said, "when it is here you've been brought?" Kamkov did not mean to be rude; he only wanted to sleep. But the man found this amusing, giving Kamkov a smile that upside down appeared to be a frown. "How can you not talk to God," he said, "when it is here you've been brought?"

Before Kamkov could answer, another voice came from their side: "Right!" And so as the prisoners flopped over, Kamkov moved with them, unable to resist letting his fingers push across his face and seek some small amount of relief.

The next morning, Kamkov was given a dull shovel and sent down into a ditch. He dug while others around him fell over and were covered with dirt, and he dug until he forgot about the weeks and the months and the whole concept of time. The one thing that remained was the stench of the barracks. It was from the *parasha*, the oil drum in the corner that was equipped with a sharpened rim and a wooden plank that lay across it. The smell was overpowering. Red Moscow, they called it, after the perfume then popular in the capital. Kamkov was sure this stench would never leave his nose, which isn't to say he wasn't sometimes thankful. When a fellow bunk-mate died, and his death needed to be hidden so his rations could be shared, then Kamkov liked to stand near the toilet and breathe deep of its fumes, to take in its stench and it alone.

One day, Kamkov was pleased to see Egnatashvili join him in the trench.

"We are digging a canal," the poet boasted.

"I do not care," Kamkov answered.

"It will greatly benefit the Soviet people."

"Then I must not be a person, or I must not be alive."

Egnatashvili laughed. Kamkov rested on the handle of his shovel and turned his eyes for a moment to the skies. So rarely did he do this, for the heavens in the day were without a star and at night the sky was hidden from him, locked away behind a padlocked door and the wooden boards across the windows.

"You!" a guard yelled, coming toward Kamkov with his dog, a German shepherd that pulled hard against its leash. "Dig!" he said, and so Kamkov dug, always he dug.

Not long after this, when the prisoners were given a free evening to celebrate the anniversary of the revolution, Egnatashvili came to Kamkov with a present. It was a branch, one as hollowed out as Kamkov felt. It was nothing, a mere pittance, Kamkov thought. He handed it back, but Egnatashvili insisted, pushing it onto his friend until in frustration Kamkov said, "What? What is it? A stick to beat myself with? What?"

Egnatashvili answered, "A telescope. It is a telescope to see through." And here he turned it to the heavens, where there were hundreds or thousands or millions of twinkling things, lights like lanterns coming through the forest from afar. "A telescope," he said.

Kamkov accepted the present a second time. A birch bark telescope as long as his arm. "Stars?" he said. "To see with?"

"A telescope," Egnatashvili agreed.

That night, Egnatashvili thought to escape – he ran to the perimeter and was shot in the back. Kamkov heard in the morning, and that night he honored his friend in a way the others thought crazy. "Stars," Kamkov said, thrusting his telescope onto first this bunk-mate and then that. "Stars," he said, but his comrades ignored him, they did that or they pointed to the ceiling, saying there were no stars, only a roof, only a roof, you fool, now sleep, sleep so we all can.

In the coming weeks, the skies grew grayer and the ground wet, and Kamkov found himself working alongside a new prisoner who identified himself as a scientist. Immediately, it was like he had returned to his old life. He couldn't stop talking, and for once he heard himself talking good sense. Through the morning and on into lunch, Kamkov talked, he talked and talked, questioning old theories and putting forth new ones, trashing the papers of rivals and praising those whose work he considered wrongly ignored. He even said at one point that he disagreed with Engels and did not consider Sir Isaac Newton "an inductive ass," though by then he realized his mistake: he had not been witty enough, nor clear enough, but most of all he had monopolized the conversation. Kamkov apologized, saying his impoliteness was only enthusiasm, and for this he was rewarded; the scientist said it was not a problem, and then took Kamkov's bowl to clean it with his in the water bucket that had been set beside their trench.

The next morning, Kamkov was awoken with a slap to the face and dragged before the warden, where his trial (and it was half over before he realized it was that) lasted less than three minutes. During this time, he was reminded that Engels was an eminent Marxist, he was asked if he would like some tea, and he was told his sentence had been upgraded to death.

"There is some paperwork required," the warden said. "A signature, a duplicate, you no doubt understand. But you should expect to be before the firing squad by the end of the month. Please do not let this affect your work. We must remember the state."

Kamkov dug alone that day, refusing to meet the eyes of anyone in his trench, especially those of the scientist who had reported him for a thicker slice of black bread. Human companionship – there was no need for it. It was only in groups that evil could be practiced; alone, it was just a theory. So Kamkov vowed, so close to death, that he would never again speak, not to anyone, not at all, not for anything. He would retreat to a world of theory, and so for that he did not even need his telescope. He would burn it in the stove; it would give them the warmth they'd need to survive the next freeze.

"You!" a guard said. "Dig!"

And so Kamkov looked up. And scowled. And nodded. And dug. But he did not speak.

The following week, Kamkov awoke with the same silent resignation he had carried with him like a sack of stones since making his vow. It was dark and cold and early. He had not been able to sleep. He swung his legs over the end of his bunk, seeing the man on the lower bunk across from him sitting in a similar way while plucking the fur of a small dog. "Shh! Shh!" the man said, looking around at all the sleeping prisoners. "It is food! Food they don't know of!" He plucked more brown fur, as if this dog were a chicken or a goose, and laughed at his good fortune. "If you don't tell the others, we will share. Would you like that? We will share!"

Silence. It was what every scientist wanted in the end. An answer to a question, an end to doubt. And so while the others awoke clutching makeshift beads or icons and muttering prayers to the gods that had been vanquished alongside the tsar, Kamkov tried to push away his thoughts until he had none, until his lips breathed silence inside and out. He believed himself talented at this, the intellectual equivalent of a saint, for several times each day he would shake his head with a start, realizing he did not know where he was, or what he was doing, and that he could not explain his actions for the last hour or more. It was ecstasy, he thought. Vanishing into himself. Disappearing while alive, living while dead. Immortality only required your ability to forget.

Once, Kamkov came out of such a trance while receiving a beating from the guards. It was most extraordinary. He did not feel the pain. Not as they kicked him, not as they punched him, not as they threw him into the mud. "Speak!" they yelled. "Talk and we'll let you go!" "Tell us your mother was a whore and you'll be spared!" But Kamkov refused. He remained silent while being thrown from one to the other and down again into the mud. He did not speak while a leashed husky came lunging and barking into his face. He kept quiet against the boots and the fists and when they urinated on his back. Yes, Kamkov did not talk. He no longer even moved. And he only betrayed the fact that he was indeed alive when he saw the madman in the door of the barracks chewing on the flesh of the dead dog's dismembered leg. Now as Kamkov lay in a puddle, his eyes were wide open, and he thought of his own lost animal. Kashtanka, where had she gone? He was ready to find out.

On the day of his execution, Kamkov stood in line counting the number of heads in front of his own: twenty. Twelve men stood in a more a decisive row off at his side, each with their hands and feet tied to a wooden pole. Then there was a crack of gunpowder and the bodies sagged forward, held up by their restraints. Just as quickly, a team of prisoners ran before the newly dead, loosening their ties and carrying the bodies away like limp and empty stretchers. The executioners took the opportunity to lower their rifles and complain about the weather (rain this morning, probably more again this afternoon) because they could not complain of the work. Kamkov heeded a guard's command to step forward, and when he stopped he counted again, in case he had been mistaken. He had not. Now there remained eight heads and no more. Kamkov looked to his left, to the twelve prisoners tied to their poles. Some squirmed at the ankles and hips, trying to break free from what bound them; one stood still and announced, "Everything for the proletariat!" Kamkov looked at the mud between his shoes, feeling something warm trickle down his legs. Then a finger poked into his chest, and looking up he saw the man in front of him smiling like a devil, a tall thin man with a shaved head and dancing eyes and cheek-bones so sharp they reminded Kamkov of cut glass.

"It is like Comrade Yagoda said," the man told him. "From Stalin I deserved gratitude for a job well done, but from God? A great punishment! And tell me, what have I received? In what line do I stand, and what shall I soon receive?"

Kamkov stared at the man. This had nothing to do with him; he was sure.

"Do you not see me?" the man said, poking his chest again. "I interrogated you! In Dmitrov jail, I wrote your confession! It was me!"

Kamkov felt something release in his stomach. *What did I not do?* He wanted desperately to know, even here, even now. *What did I not do?* But he had not spoken in weeks, in months perhaps, and after so much silence he could not speak, even here, even now.

"For years I wrote such confessions," the man continued. "My wife sometimes even. We would lie awake in bed thinking of ways others could be counter-revolutionaries." He laughed, the sound sharp and hollow, and Kamkov was reminded of the village lunatic of his youth, a man who'd frightened him most when he'd enjoyed a moment's sanity. "The walls were thin," he whispered. "My neighbors heard us and thought we were Old Leninists plotting against the regime. So tell me, is there a god? For here I am about to receive this" – his arm went out at the sound of the executioners reloading their rifles – "while from Stalin I should be receiving a promotion for my years of honorable service."

The bullets rang out, the twelve men fell dead, and the prisoners on work-detail rushed in to take the bodies away. "God?" Kamkov said, and like that he was pulled from the line, away from the agent who had questioned him, away from the others, and away from his death. He was twenty feet further on before he saw who had grabbed him – a guard – and where they were going – to the warden, who stood in the shadows of the watchtower. When they reached him, the guard pulled sharply on the back of Kamkov's shirt, halting their advance.

"You have been rehabilitated," the warden said. "You are to report to the Moscow Planetarium—"

"The Moscow Planetarium?" For this was like a promotion.

The warden nodded, and spoke as if having conveniently forgotten the pertinent details of Kamkov's file. "Due to the many disgraces last year in Leningrad," he said, "several scientists have been reassigned from the capital. You are now needed to fill one of these vacancies. So" – he thrust some papers into Kamkov's hands – "the guard will point you in the direction of the train."

On that, Kamkov was pulled away by the shirt, hearing the rifles release behind him. He struggled to look over his shoulder, finding the wooden pole that was the ninth from the left. He could not see the face of the man who had taken his place and his bullet (his chin was down against his chest) and so he looked to the skies for something else.

The guard released him at the gate and pointed. "Go," he said, and so Kamkov did. He walked, and then ran, and then fell to his knees and brought the mud up to his cheeks, rubbing it into his skin like a holy water or a healing salve. After so much silence, even his crying did not make a sound. So he sat there silently sobbing and flailing about in the mud, looking like nothing more than a man whose voice had not yet reached this world.

Kamkov bathed in a creek, washing his face and arms and chest, and then he walked toward the horizon, down a muddy road that bled into a muddier field in which nothing grew taller than a child. His head was like a box of silence, and when he found himself inside the train station, he stared dumbly at the woman behind the ticket counter.

"Where are you going?" she said, and when Kamkov continued to stare, she asked him again, and he mouthed the last word he had been able to say aloud, the one that now seemed to be the only word appropriate: God. He was a man of science, and he feared he was a believer. So when the woman said he had to speak up, that she could not hear him, Kamkov said the word aloud – "God" – and as he did he felt its power push all throughout his body, as if he had been building a dam with his silence and this word was its crack.

For a little more than a month, Kamkov worked at his new post in Moscow. Then Stalin called, asking for clarification on a matter of celestial importance, and Kamkov awoke to the sound of a knock. Instinctively, he reached for his cross, the one he wore around his neck when he was alone at home. Each night that he put it on the silver felt cold against his chest, and each morning he took it off feeling the warmth of his body. He clutched it now, blinking until he felt suitably sure he had not heard what he had heard. Then the knock returned, again so softly it sounded like nothing more than his fears.

"Kamkov?" a voice said. "Kamkov, are you there?"

The secret police were changing, he thought. They were developing the more psychological aspects of torture to go along with their ready mastery of the stick and the boot.

"Kamkov?" the voice said. "Will you open up? Please?"

Please? They were asking politely now! "Who is it?" he said. "What have I done?"

"It is not what you think," the voice returned.

Kamkov turned and looked to a photograph he'd pinned above his headboard. It was not one of his own dog, but it was a Yorkshire terrier and it reminded him of Kashtanka all the same. Kamkov glanced from it to a clock on the bedside table. It was a little after four – late for the night life, but perhaps they had been busy and this was the end of their shift. "If it is not what I think," he said, "then I do not know what to think. And if I do not know what to think, I do not think I should open the door."

Kamkov heard a thump, but it was not from the force of a fist or a foot; it was the sound of a head falling forward. "Kamkov," the man pleaded. "You do not understand. It is my first day. I wasn't supposed to start until morning, but the director calls and wakes me. It is a very important job, he says. And I am alone. You must help. I was trained as a cobbler, and my wife..."

Kamkov stood and scratched at his pajama bottoms. "Help?" It was what Christ wanted. He had read of this and other things in the book he kept under his mattress. And so was that why they were here? To take away his words as they had taken away his dog and his stars? "Have I committed another crime?" he said.

"No!"

"Because if I have, I'd like to know what exactly I did, and how exactly I came to do it." He glanced to his photo, nodding as if to agree with the dog that this was a job well done. "These things are important. To know what you have not done."

"Your presence has been requested by Stalin," the man at the door said. "The Great Leader would like to know" – but he could not finish. Kamkov opened the door, causing the agent of the People's Commissariat for Internal Affairs to fall forward into his arms.

"Stalin, did you say?" It was like receiving an invitation from God, or at least his closest competitor. With it, Kamkov could know the answers, or at least better understand the question: How? And whether or not he was now a believer, he most certainly remained one thing: a scientist. And for a scientist there was nothing better. "Stalin?"

The agent regained his posture and averted his eyes from Kamkov's face, which was spotted with the fleshy red scars that remained from his night in the box. "Yes," he said. "It is Stalin himself who has called."

"And you're not going to arrest me?"

"No."

It still made no sense. "Then why come at this hour?"

"Because it is at this hour that Stalin has asked his question."

"But why not call on Dmitri?" Kamkov said. "He lives closer to the planetarium than I."

The agent looked over Kamkov's shoulder. His voice fell to a whisper. "Dmitri must have seen my car through his window. A neighbor said he had not been sleeping well since …"

Kamkov nodded. The purge of the Pulkovo Observatory. He did not need to hear.

"So he jumped," the secret policeman said. "As I walked up the five flights of stairs, Dmitri jumped."

"He is dead?"

The young agent would only repeat himself. "Dmitri jumped."

After a moment, Kamkov found the courage to go on. "And Viktor? Who lives just two blocks from him?"

"Also dead."

"But his apartment is on the ground floor."

"And when he answered and saw who I was he fled up the stairs to find a window of a more desirable height. I did not have time to explain."

Kamkov shook his head until he remembered the next name. "Boris?"

The agent walked to Kamkov's bed, where he sat and put his head in his hands. "He fell into my arms after opening the door. He clutched his heart and said he was too old for the camps and too weak for the torture. I held him like a baby as his eyes rolled into the back of his head." The agent's stomach quivered as he breathed uneasily through his nose. "Please do not speak to anyone of what I tell you. I beg you. I should not be talking, but I don't officially start this job until morning and already I feel responsible for the lives of three men. I am a cobbler by training, this is my first night." He looked up. Kamkov stood over him. "My first night and now I am late, so late to bring you before Stalin I do not dare think what he will do. My wife," he said. "You must help."

Kamkov reached to the foot of his bed for his trousers. He put them on and from the front pocket took out a pack of cigarettes. The agent accepted one and stood as Kamkov extended a light.

"I will help you," Kamkov said. "Do you hear? I can help you." And he smiled, as if trying to convince the man of what he'd almost convinced himself. "God exists," he said. "Did you know that? I have felt His presence and know He exists."

The agent smoked, looking to the thin walls around them. "That may be so," he whispered. "But Stalin exists as well, and it is he who knows where I live."

While pulling up to the dacha, after twice taking the wrong farming road and twice fearing he was lost, the agent asked of Kamkov a favor.

"If he is not too angry, perhaps you could speak to him about the difficulties I encountered? And how I could not control them?"

Kamkov assured the man he would, but only after convincing him to reveal his name: Sergei Pavlovich Platov.

"I thank you," Platov said. "You are a great man, and for this I will owe you my life."

"You will owe me nothing," Kamkov answered, "if you will promise to remember but one thing: That we owe our lives to each other, not ourselves. This is how we honor God."

Platov said he would wait in the car.

When Kamkov was shown into the study by a drowsy secretary, Kaganovich, asleep in his chair, responded with a gulping snore. Behind him, Stalin and Molotov stood over a table littered with papers. They looked up from their work as if trying to remember if they'd requested this interruption or if they should be upset.

"Of course," Molotov remembered. "The astronomer."

"Yes." Stalin nodded. "Kamkov the astronomer, good."

The secretary disappeared with a gracious smile, and then Kamkov took the initiative to step further into the room. "I understand there is a matter regarding the stars?"

"Precisely." Molotov marched to Kaganovich and woke him with a shove. "The astronomer is here!"

"Cassiopeia!" he growled.

Molotov turned to Kamkov with a grin. "And I say Orion. But here. You are to decide."

Molotov led them to the far window, where he pulled back the curtains and pushed out the glass. Stalin and Kaganovich crowded around him, looking first left and then right, as if to follow the movement the stars might have taken during the night. Throughout, Kamkov stood between them and looked out at a sky that was pink and blue and most certainly not black.

Stalin turned to the astronomer, lifting his mustache with a smile. "So tell me," he said, "which is it? What do you see? Cassiopeia or Orion?"

"I am sure I could not say."

"Could not?" answered Stalin. "But are not our astronomers the best in the world? Here, look closely." He pointed out the window, smiling again. "And tell me which it is."

Kamkov knew the truth and also the right answer, and he knew that they were not the same. Still, he could not lie. To do so would be like saying he was in the service of another, and he was not in the service of Stalin. So he spoke from his heart and not from his head, fearing he would lose the one he did not use. "It is neither. Neither Cassiopeia nor Orion. It is dawn, and there are no stars over Moscow."

Stalin wrinkled his narrow brow. "No stars over Moscow?"

Kamkov swallowed dryly. "We will have to wait for the heavens to once again favor us with their presence."

Molotov watched Stalin watching Kamkov. Kaganovich lifted one foot off the floor, as if ready to fly up through the ceiling. Then Stalin's belly lifted with a laugh. "Dawn! The astronomer says dawn! Of course it is!" And like that he was off, striding stiffly to his desk, with Molotov and Kaganovich following and Kaganovich crying that this did not settle it, not at all, they would have to wait for another night and call on the astronomer again.

Stalin's voice came next, ordering Kamkov to his desk. "Here." He pulled a pencil away from a piece of paper and sent the document to the bottom of a pile of papers as he thrust them into Kamkov's hands. "Have the man who drove you deliver them to Comrade Beria."

The leader of the secret police. Kamkov nodded, feeling the emptiness in his stomach and the weight in his knees. "Yes," he said. "Yes, of course."

Stalin blindly extended a hand toward the door. "You may leave."

As he emerged from the dacha, Kamkov was met by Sergei Platov, who rushed around to the passenger side of the car to open Kamkov's door. "What did Stalin say?" he asked. "Did he understand? Were you able to tell him the delay was beyond my control?"

Kamkov assured him he had, and got into the car realizing this was a man who could help him, a man who could move his name from one list to another, or erase it altogether. "You are fine," he said, as Platov sank into the seat beside him. "He even complimented your work, saying your perseverance is to be praised."

Platov could not believe it, which is to say that he did. He slapped Kamkov's thigh and pinched his cheek, thanking his new friend and telling him, "You must be right. There is a God, regardless of this Stalin." He laughed, then, and placed his foot on the gas, accelerating away from the dacha's front gate. "Let me repay you," he said. "Come eat with us tonight, you must at least give me the pleasure of that. My wife, you would be amazed at what she can do in the kitchen – she is remarkable, I tell you, truly she is!"

Kamkov nodded absently, letting his mind drift to the thought of Svetlana Borshchagovskaya, the one he had wanted to leave work with, the one who had pledged even her sex to the state. He had not seen her since being taken to the Dmitrov jail. The women had gone to one room, the men to another, no different than church. He looked now to Platov, this man who was so lucky to have avoided the camps and experienced the pleasures of a woman. Then he glanced down at the papers in his lap, still not brave enough to read what he held. Would Platov have a child? he wondered. Or perhaps he already did. Kamkov could not ask him to risk losing that, not when he himself did not even have a dog. So in the end it came down to this: the science of biology and the simplicity of math. There was more of Platov than there was of Kamkov, and that was all that mattered, list or not.

Kamkov was ready. He fixed his eyes on what he held, some ten pages or more of typed names and addresses, and brought the last page up to the top, seeing on it a stain left by a splatter of tea. The final entry had been added in pencil, and when he ran his index finger across it – Kamkov the astronomer, Moscow Planetarium – he felt what it is like to be already dead.

THE SECRET MEETING OF THE SECRET POLICE

We were parked across the street from an apartment building in central Moscow, half-heartedly observing the movements of a dissident physicist or peddler of blue-jeans – it is so long ago now, I can't even remember – when Vasily opened the back door of our car and slid into place behind us.

"Drive," he said, jabbing a finger into the air. "We're already late."

I looked at Sergei in the passenger seat, but he had grown apathetic from all of Gorbachev's talk of *glasnost* and *perestroika*. He shrugged and returned his eyes to the *Wall Street Journal* he'd stolen from the hotel room of an American businessman. "A Delaware Corporation," he read aloud, practicing his English.

I pulled out onto the road and looked for Vasily in my rear-view mirror. "What are we late for?"

"The meeting."

"Whose meeting?"

"The Secret Police."

"The Secret Police? How come I didn't know?"

"It's a secret meeting," he said.

This stirred Sergei. He half-turned in his seat. "A secret meeting of the secret police?"

Again, Vasily pointed. "Drive."

He led us to a dacha in the country at the end of a long forested road lined by cars that grew shinier and more expensive the closer they were to the front door. We were the last to arrive. By the time we pushed into the mudroom, agents were everywhere – in the kitchen, the dining room, the doors to the bedrooms and even out on the back deck.

"He is starting," a man at the far door called out to us, before relaying the Colonel General's words for us and all the others too far away to hear. "He says while the imperialists have used computers for years to increasing power and effectiveness, we at first treated them like fancy typewriters or expensive adding machines."

I nodded, throwing an arm up around Sergei's far shoulder. "It is just like you said. The capitalists are always having you buy something, thinking it is something else. When really it is the same thing sold twice, a calculator and a typewriter."

This was not exactly what he had said, but it was what I wanted to believe. That afternoon, before Vasily arrived, Sergei had pointed at the apartment building we were observing and told me that one day it would be privatized and renamed Sunshine Manor. "It will be purchased by" – and here he had consulted his newspaper to practice the new cluster of words – "a consortium of private developers and turned into up-market, live-work lofts." He had found that newspaper in January. Now, some eight months later, it was bloated from use, its pages stained by the rings of the teacups and vodka glasses he drank from while studying its propaganda each night. What else could I have thought? We had been soldiers together. He was my best friend.

Vasily slapped Sergei on the back, snorting in agreement at what I had said. "Yes. The Americans will do anything for a dollar, even drill a hole through the earth and sell it as, how do you say it? A doughnut."

There was great laughter at this, all around. It was like it had been in the sixties and seventies and even the eighties, when we still thought we were winning. But then the man at the door was calling back to us again, this time asking for Vasily.

"The Colonel General," he said, "he wants you."

Vasily acted as if he had expected nothing less. He smoothed down the front of his jacket and moved through the parting crowd. Sergei and I shared a quick look of surprise, and then we followed him before the bodies of our comrades could fall in behind him to form a wall.

The Colonel General stood in front of the fireplace, and welcomed our friend with a hug and a kiss on both cheeks. "This, comrades," the Colonel General announced, "is the man who has saved our way of life."

Vasily looked appropriately abashed. He raised his hands over the crowd's clapping and hoots of approval. "Please," he said, "please. Had you been given my most recent assignment and learned what I learned, it would be you up here talking, not me."

He was so humble. I realized then that he was a great man, perhaps a future Secretary General of the Party. It was what I had once secretly dreamed of, when I was a child still under Stalin. But this had changed when I got married. Then my dreams were only for a larger apartment, or failing that, for my wife's father and brother to fall asleep with their backs to us more often, allowing Liliya and I to make love.

"Gorbachev can't be trusted!"

"He works for the CIA!"

"Please, please!" Vasily was bouncing his hands in the air before him. "You are right, all of you. We have our reasons to be suspicious." I turned nodding sharply to those agents around me, pausing here and there when others nodded no less vehemently at me. "But only recently have we learned of a technology Gorbachev covets and hopes to implement," Vasily continued. "It is a technology that will take your job, and yours – all of ours," he said, sweeping his hand across the room. "It is a technology that will be the end of the secret police as we know it."

It was as if a giant rock had fallen from space, silencing us beneath its weight and gravity.

"What is it, Vasily?"

It was Sergei talking, sounding more curious than afraid, as he often did when reciting passages from his newspaper. *Angel investor. Ownership equity. Start up funding.*

"Speak to us of this technology," he said.

Vasily did, but first he waited, as if considering the possibility that the word, once released, would rouse Lenin from his sleep and send him barreling out of his tomb.

"It is called the Internet."

The following afternoon, my wife and I stood in a line that stretched for three blocks.

"You do not understand," I said. "It could be very dangerous."

Liliya stepped forward, and I stepped with her. "Dangerous?" she said. "What danger? From what you tell me I could read the newspapers from America."

I grabbed her arm above the elbow and pulled her close to speak into her ear. "Why would you read the papers from America?"

She shook my hand free and spoke louder, though I had whispered. "To know what is happening there," she said. "Only by knowing what is happening there can I understand what is happening here."

An old man turned round to face us, having heard my wife's foolish talk. He stood two spots forward, wearing a brown overcoat that was pulling apart at one shoulder.

"Listen," I said, still speaking to my wife with a whisper, "this Internet, it will have a surveillance system. Vasily said all the thoughts in your brain, all your wants and desires, will be filtered through it and reported to the government. The state will use this information to its advantage – it always does. And so if you do not see the danger in that, then I do not know why I tell you anything."

My wife stepped forward in line. I stepped with her.

"It will put me out of a job," I said finally. "Will you like that? I will wake up one day and be a postman. Do you hear?"

My wife would not answer. The only one who would listen was the old man in the brown overcoat. "What is your name?" I said, my voice a bark that spoke of my profession. "Tell me your name and address, where you live!"

He turned back around, and my wife looked at me as if I had shot him.

"What?" I asked.

She pursed her lips, stepping forward with the line. After a moment she asked, "You could do the shopping from this Internet? Without leaving the home?"

"Yes," I told her. "I believe so."

"Sausages? I could buy sausages?"

"Everything," I said, though with little remaining patience. I did not wish to discuss it anymore, least of all in public. "You could buy everything, sausages if you wish, but this is only so the capitalists will be convinced to bring the system into their homes."

The woman directly in front of us turned round and asked, "What is this thing you speak of? This Internet that lets you shop from the home for sausages?"

My wife leaned forward and whispered in her ear, and while she did I looked to all the others, to the front and to the rear, who seemed only to be interested in us. There was no point in hiding it anymore.

"I married an enemy of the state," I said. "Do you see? Can't you hear? She wishes to read the papers from America and to buy sausages in her *khalat*."

"It would be better than being all day in a line," my wife said, to which the woman in front of us nodded, adding that it is impossible to do all the cooking when you are doing so much of the standing. "And we must work in the factories and at the home," she finished, to which the old man in the overcoat swatted the air, saying, "Bah! This *glasnost*, bah!"

I glared at Liliya, though she would not acknowledge me. "I should have married Kseniya," I muttered. "The simple girl from across the hall, when I was a child. She needed help in the bathroom, but was very loving, very warm. With her I could have made a happy life. How she loved my mother's cabbage. But you."

My wife stepped forward and I stepped with her. Then finally we were at the front and I was asking what we had been waiting for. It did not matter. There was none left.

"But you may have this ticket," the woman behind the counter told us. "It allows you to stand in a different line tomorrow, one for the people who stood in the line today."

"And what will be at the front of that one?"

"If you are lucky," she said, "not another ticket."

My wife turned to me, then, and before she walked off, not even waiting for me to join her, she said, "Sausages. What I would give for just a pot of sausages."

Six days later, it was my great honor to place the knock on President Mikhail Sergeyevich Gorbachev's door while he vacationed at his dacha in the Crimea.

"Who is it?" he said.

And I answered, "The State Committee for the State of Emergency in the Union of Soviet Socialist Republics."

We heard footsteps across the wooden floor, and then the door swung open on the President, who held in one hand the treaty that would soon grant the union's fifteen republics their independence. He looked at the four men gathered behind me, among them his chief-of-staff, Valery Boldin. "I did not authorize a State Committee for the State of Emergency," he said, and Comrade Boldin nodded slowly, as if this was a most regrettable oversight. "What do you want?" The President retreated to his desk, where he lifted one of the five phones arranged there. It was dead, just like all the others. He turned to us. "What do you want?"

Comrade Boldin stepped forward, pulling a twelve-page document from his attaché case. "A signature, Comrade Gorbachev, that is all." He laid the referendum on the desk. "It declares a state of emergency, and authorizes several reform measures. It is needed. If you were not so sick, you would understand."

"Sick? I am not sick."

The chief-of-staff smiled politely. "You have serious health problems."

"Health problems? You're mad. All of you."

Comrade Boldin picked up the referendum and held it out for Gorbachev. "If you do not sign, Vice President Yanayev assumes control. The troops are already on the move."

Gorbachev started for the door. "Where is Raisa? What have you done with my wife?"

But with a look from Comrade Boldin (it was clear he would not sign) I stepped forward and punched the President in the solar plexus, taking all of his air. Gorbachev slumped to the floor, the treaty falling at his side. One of the agents hurried over and pressed a napkin to the President's mouth and nose – chloroform. A second picked up a black briefcase he found resting against the foot of a chair.

"Bring that," Comrade Boldin said, closing his attaché case on the referendum. "It contains the launch codes."

Gorbachev was now as limp as a newspaper made wet by the rain. I directed a final agent to get his feet, and then squatted down to pick him up at the shoulders.

"Let's carry him into the living room," I said. "There is a TV in there."

The next morning, the news agency TASS announced that Yanayev had assumed control because Gorbachev had "serious health problems." It was also announced that all demonstrations and strikes were banned, and that the media were under government control.

I was not with Yanayev in Moscow when he received the call from Boris Yeltsin, who apparently had been on the phone all day with a number of world leaders, even the Americans. But when Yanayev called Gorbachev's dacha shortly thereafter, and I mistakenly took the initiative to answer the ringing, I did learn what the Vice-President had told him: "We don't accept your gang of bandits!"

"Who was supposed to arrest Yeltsin?" Yanayev asked me. "Who?! Who has forgotten him and bungled the coup?"

I looked at the TV, which was tuned to CNN. Yeltsin stood atop a tank, calling on the Soviet people to rise up in solidarity against our take-over. Twenty thousand people were gathered before him, pushing in amongst our troops as he waved the flag of the old Russian empire, its colors red, white, and blue. I felt sick to my stomach as I thought of Sergei, who was good with a knife and had been assigned the task with two other men. I wondered what he'd done with their bodies, and if perhaps he was already in the crowd – perhaps there alongside my own wife.

I sank into a seat against the wall, hearing his voice in my head. *Filed for Chapter 13 Bankruptcy. Once we complete our financial restructuring.*

I gave my apologies to Yanayev and said I accepted full responsibility. "I should have known," I told him. "He hasn't been himself." Then we hung up and I returned to the sofa in the living room, where President Gorbachev sat eating an apple.

"What is this Internet?" I asked him. "Is it really what they say?"

"It is the future," the President said. "We cannot ignore it any longer, so we had better embrace it."

"And people will really use it?" I said. "They will expose their political leanings, their sexual deviancies, and send mail that can be intercepted without their even realizing it? You are telling me people will do this, not suspecting the technology will be used against them?"

Gorbachev bit into the apple and chewed. "People will use it," he said, giving a bounce to the apple in his hand, "and they will even pay as much as fifteen-hundred rubles per month for the privilege. It will be revolutionary. The state will be able to police its citizens for kopeks on the ruble what it costs today." He looked to the TV and watched Yeltsin waving that flag to the crowd's delight. "It will be like the olden times. If there is dissent, it will not last. We will be able to kick down doors without even leaving the office."

I shook my head, and fell back into the cushions of the sofa. What did this coup matter? Time had already passed me by. I looked at myself as you do a memory.

"And then there will be phones," Gorbachev continued, speaking to me like a great mystic. "Phones," he said, "that people will carry with them at all times. They will be connected to a system of surveillance towers, allowing the police to know where you are even when you are quiet and alone. It is amazing what the future holds, Yuri, and how the people will embrace it." He turned to me, then, adding tenderly, almost apologetically, that if there is a new fascism, it will not be the result of a bloody coup. "It will be paid for in monthly installments," he said. "Do you hear me? Monthly installments, Yuri."

I nodded weakly, looking back to Yeltsin on the TV. It was more of the same, and I was already too late. So I sat there, waiting for the knock.

THE CASTRATO OF ST. PETERSBURG

1.

Since coming to land of the tsar, I have allowed myself to be known as the Castrato of St. Petersburg. You would find no such willingness among those of my mixed sex who tour the courts of Europe using their lofty voices for profit and pride. They would have you believe their talent God-given, not the consequence of a barber-surgeon's hand, and if ever you dared to say otherwise – that an earthly butcher froze their voice in place, perhaps at the urging of their own father – you would be paid for it with their fists and their feet and the most dizzying screams of their fury. I know. I was once the same. But now I am older – and wiser, I tell myself – so if you see me walking the banks of the Neva, call me what you wish. Castrato. *Non integri*. These taunts and whispers hold no power anymore. I gut them as if they were one of my father's pigs, and turn them into something as fine as his famous salami.

Before coming to this cold northern land I knew many other names. At the baptismal I was Petrus Augostino Benedetto. On the stage, Norcinelli. And in my marriage bed, a place so few of us castrati go, It's-All-Right. Mine has been a full life, I know, and still my years are perhaps only half spent. The tsar's doctors have assured me of this. After Bourgeois the Giant died, and his skeletal remains were placed in the glass coffin that stands in the center of the room in which I write, a team of medical men completed a thorough investigation of my health and concluded I should see another two decades or three. They are years I will cherish. But also years when I will continue to hear that one name I've never eluded, "fool." Or as we said it in my former land, "pantaloun."

The first I heard such a curse was the summer I turned nine, when with my three brothers I went kicking a ball through the dust in town. It got away from us and my twin ran to collect it, giving me a moment to read a sign that hung over the shadow of an open door. *Castration, Quick and Cheap.* We in Norcia were kind to our pigs, I thought. They gave us the ham and prosciutto and salami that was served on the finest tables between here and Assisi, and for this we repaid them by making sure their pain was brief. I told this to my brothers as my twin returned with the ball, and they laughed and pushed me around between them, saying I was an imbecile if I believed they castrated only pigs. "He is Pantaloun!" shouted my twin, always playing up to the others. "Pantaloun!" And he hopped away like the character famous to the Venetian stage, a man who covered his skinny legs with knee-breeches so tight he could only walk with the type of short quick steps that come when your feet are bare and the ground is hot. "Pantaloun!" he repeated, hopping all over. "Our Brother Pantaloun!"

I thought the very best, and for this I earned their names and laughter. My mother said not to worry. She told me I was strangely blessed. "God breathes into each of us at birth. He presses His lips to our own," she said, "and gives us the faith and goodness we will need in life. But I am sure He grew confused when I had you boys, for it seems He filled your lungs twice and your brother's not at all." My twin was so cagey he doubted even the moon. "It is full and hangs over your shoulder!" I told him one night in the field. "Look! You will never see the likes of it again!" But he would not glance up, would only turn his eyes to mine in a way that said he had discovered my trick and would not let it play out. A different kind of fool, I have come to think. The one who refuses to be fooled at all.

I began to think of all this again recently, when a touring menagerie came to my new home in Petersburg. The company's posters quickly went up in all the most fashionable districts, urging passersby to *See the fiercest apes of Africa!* and *View the savage grace of these deadly beasts!* The first poster I came upon was on Nevsky Prospekt, glued over another directing people to *The Castrato of St. Petersburg – performing daily at The Kuntskamera.* So I am no different than a monkey, I thought. It would have made Galterio weep, it would have sent Ridolfo into a rage. But such thinking is how we sin against our faith, and soon I rediscovered mine, the faith that says mine is a happy story, complete with a happy end. You may disagree. You may hear what follows and cast me in that familiar role of the fool once more. But only God can judge us so.

Let me begin.

It has been twenty years since I was taken over the high mountains surrounding my childhood home, long enough to believe that my father and mother are dead and the three sons they kept have had sons and perhaps even sons of sons. My last night in Norcia, or the night I last remember myself as Petrus Augostino Benedetto, I sat in my chair at the dinner table, only to have its four legs splinter and crack, dropping me with a curse to the floor. My father was the only one not to laugh. He stood shaking his spoon as if I'd done this trick to complicate his digestion.

"Must you always perform?" he said. "What is it that brings out the fool in you?"

I was still young enough to believe every question demanded an answer, so I stood there holding one of the chair's legs and wearing a grave expression. My father had recently begun to shape and polish olive branches. He gave them seats of tightly woven string with hopes he could leave the fields behind and enter town as an artisan. But if his creations could not hold me and I was only ninety pounds, how to tell him he was no more a carpenter than I a fool? In the end it did not matter, for as soon as I opened my mouth to speak he cursed my silence and pulled me up by my ear.

"You wish to entertain, you fool?" He slapped me so hard I swung like the bells of St. Benedict. "Then sing, Petrus! Sing while the rest of us eat!"

And so I sang. As my father's chair creaked beneath his weight and the crackling of the fire returned to my now-ringing ear, I sang while clasping my hands beneath my chin, first those religious chants that were as familiar to me as my mother's voice, and then portions of an aria I'd heard performed by a traveling player in town. My eyes I kept closed, but I imagined my father's look of enchantment, for I had come upon it many times in the hills, when I would trail behind the sheep he led and sing the animals toward the pasture. "To look at you," he once said, "one would think you sing to breathe."

I only opened my eyes when my twin brother shook me by the shoulder; it was then that I saw my eldest brother shuttering the window – it had banged open with the wind – and my father speaking with a stranger at the door. The stranger wore a long yellow coat and a matching vest lined with pearl buttons. His hat had three corners and his long black leather gloves matched the color of his boots, which had lost their polish in the rain.

"I was sure it was the voice of an angel," the man said. "I had to stop my horse and see." He looked over my father's shoulder, then – he stood a good half-foot taller than him – and I saw for the first time his nose, a crooked thing that turned back on itself like a river that had lost faith in its direction.

Our home was but a single room with a single window and a single door, but my father said if we only had a single bowl of soup, our guest would be given no less than our biggest spoon. My mother took the man's coat and hung it at my back by the fire; my father pulled out his chair for the guest and brushed its seat with his hand. The stranger thanked him with a smile, and said he was from Russia and worked as a cultural ambassador for the tsar. My mother flushed, telling my brothers to sit up. "Forgive the lentil soup," she told the stranger. "If only you had come tomorrow, when the beans would be softer and the ham not so hard."

The stranger held up his palm and smiled like a painting in our church. "Madam, I travel back and forth across Europe, securing my master's many wishes. But even if I had stopped tonight in the court of a queen, it is not possible that I could have found hospitality equal to this. So please, if it helps you," and here his smile widened beneath his crooked nose, "consider me only a poor stranger who is well-dressed."

My father glanced over his shoulder, told my mother not to interrupt, and then the stranger was continuing. He told us that in his many travels he had learned seven languages, a thought so wild to me that I lost myself imagining the seven countries home to these seven tongues. I reached no further than six, and this only after remembering the Portuguese, before the man pushed his bowl to the center of the table and complimented my mother on the softness of her beans.

She blushed. My father sat back in his chair.

"But tell me, what does your tsar send you for this time?" My father half-rose from his chair. "*Sausage?*" He had some hanging in the shed.

Again the Russian raised his hand, this time while consulting a silver pocket-watch he fished from his vest. "*When* did the tsar send me would be a better question." He snapped the watch closed and looked around the table. "My travels have been long and not without complication, least of all in Württemberg." He swatted the air. "But this is of no concern to you. The tsar seeks" – here he paused. "I only know how to say it in Russian," he explained. "But perhaps it is still familiar to you." He said the word – *kastraty* – and gave an apologetic look to my mother before continuing. "It is the type of singer for which Norcia is fast becoming known, and I see that not only are you well-blessed..." He looked from my one brother to the next, ending with a reconfirming glance between me and my twin. "You even have a spare."

My father glanced over his shoulder to my mother, who stood behind him, holding onto the back of his chair. She looked to my brothers, who dropped their eyes over their bowls. No one looked at the stranger but me.

"He is the youngest?"

"By seven minutes," my father said.

I stood still before the fire, glancing around the table, the splintered wood at my feet and a leg of the broken chair in my hands. There was no place to sit.

My father leaned toward the stranger. "We are a humble family of humble means. However much we would like to help, we cannot even afford to give a son to the Church."

The Russian drank a gulp of wine. "Of course. Of course," he said. "But you know a servant to the tsar is very comfortable? So comfortable, in fact, that his family finds comfort too."

My father pursed his lips. "But for what kind of life?" he asked, adding with a whisper, "These men, they do not know women."

The Russian laughed. "They do not? I must tell Ridolfo!" He set his cup down, splashing wine onto the table. "Or did you not hear the commotion he caused last year in Rome?"

My father knew Ridolfo as we all did, but he betrayed no expression.

"His gilded carriage was mobbed on its way to the Vatican. He was scheduled to perform for the Pope, but his driver had to stop every two-hundred meters to clear the women from the road." My brothers looked up from their bowls. "For every two ladies that fainted, one was found with a medallion round her neck that bore a portrait of the singer's face. So do not believe those who say Ridolfo is more mouth than man. Who else among us travels with four escorts to keep the women he does not know from those he does?" His chin dropped into his neck. "And remember, his love for women never wakes him nine months later with a cry and another hungry mouth to feed."

My father looked for a long time at the stranger, and the stranger looked for a long time at him. Neither seemed willing to move or speak. The only sound came from the fire behind me, the flames crackling as they ate into the wood. My father looked at my mother. Her eyes fell to the splintered wood between my ankles. I had this thought: I could rebuild the chair, and take my seat at the table alongside my brothers, and –

My father leaned toward the stranger until they were close enough to kiss. "Tell me, why would the tsar look to my home for a singer of this type if his empire is larger than any I know? The people of my land are gifted with song, this is true, but in Russia is there not one talented boy who could have kept you from tiring your horse?"

The Russian nodded. "But you must understand, the tsar is a Christian man, and Russia a Christian nation. To look inside our borders" – he pursed his lips and shook his head – "would be to invite a blasphemy on our soil."

My father's face flushed until I saw the lines of blood in his neck. "But we are Christians too, and the Pope himself has said it is allowed so long as the child sings for the glory of God."

The Russian nodded briskly as if he'd heard all this before and believed it true himself.

"Yet your tsar considers it no blasphemy to find a singer elsewhere and invite him into his court?"

The Russian ran a thumb and forefinger down the sides of his nose, as if trying to straighten it. "A Good Christian cannot with clear conscience commit a crime against God. But he can discover one. In fact, he must, it is his duty, for then he can show it his Christian charity."

My father looked away, snorting.

The Russian smiled and made the sign of the cross over his lips. "It takes the mind of God to understand the laws of man."

Again, they did not move or speak, just looked at each other in a silence that left me weak in the knees. I turned and placed the broken leg of the chair in the fire, and at that moment the door blew open with the wind. My eldest brother stood to shut it, but my father rose and waved him back into his seat. "Come," he said, and the Russian followed him to the door, where they spoke in hushed tones. My father's voice rose. The Russian pulled him further into the cold, the wind now blowing at their hair. My mother stoked the fire and I looked to the stranger's seat wondering if I might take it for myself. But then my father turned inside with a stiff clap of his hands. "Boys!" he said. "Come with us to the barn."

My father and the Russian led the way, each holding a lantern as they crossed the field. My brothers and I followed according to age, and though my twin had beat me into this world by only seven minutes, I was left one step outside the circles of light.

Inside the barn, my father hung the lanterns from a hooked beam and gave directions: my middle brother was to take the Russian's overcoat and drape it over the horse's stall, the eldest was to milk the cow, and my twin should hurry to the well. "Take this bucket," he said. "And warm the contents indoors." I was still waiting to receive instructions of my own when my father turned away with the Russian, the two of them moving now toward the metal basin in which my family bathed. When they had reached it, the Russian rolled up his sleeves and my father stood with his hands on his hips. They were half-lost to me in the shadows, their voices only fully reclaimed after all these years and so many nights of imagining.

"And you are sure he has the talent for it?"

"Each castrato is born to sing a song," the Russian answered.

"But there are more every day, and surely not all can sing the same."

The Russian did not answer, for what could he say? This was true. When Pietro Paolo Folignati and Girolamo Rossini had been entered into the registry of the Papal Choir, the castrati had been as rare as the days when the moon blotted out the sun. But now all the best houses of *opera seria* advertised a castrato in the lead, and the most famous of these performers traveled as far as London. There were so many singers the butchers of our town had indeed become famous. He was bitten by a pig, fathers would explain after leaving these houses of slaughter. Or they would insist their son was a natural castrato, born to bless the world with his song.

"I can tell you only this," the Russian at last said, "I am the cultural attaché of His Grand Eminence The Tsar. To question me is to question him, and to question him is to question He who put him on the throne."

My father stood there silently. He was a religious man. And he had said it so many times: I sang as if to breathe.

"You could say," the Russian continued, "your son's talent is without question."

"But should we wait till morning at least, to visit the man I know in town? He is my friend and I hear his hand is steady. I can trust him to give us his word. No one will know."

The Russian spoke quickly. "It is not necessary. I am trained in all manner of ways. Your son will be fine, and I do think it best we avoid the light of day."

My father relented with a nod – it is hard not to agree with a man who stands so much taller than you – and they shuffled toward me with the basin. "There's one more thing," the Russian said, his voice strained by the weight of what they carried. My father needed no further prompting. After they set the basin down, he reached inside his shirt for the small leather pouch he wore around his neck and removed several heavy coins.

"I apologize again," the Russian said.

My father nodded and counted out the last of the coins into his hand.

"These highwaymen in Württemberg, they took from me not just my gold, but the silver cross that hung from my neck – my grandmother's cross." He reached for what was no longer there. "You must understand."

My father said he did, of course. The money was for my benefit. It would pay for my meals en route to The Winter Palace in Petersburg, then be returned with the first installment of my salary – money given to me when I was receiving the finest education and training.

My eldest brother arrived at our side to empty his bucket. The milk streamed into the basin and splashed up onto my face. The Russian disappeared with my father into the shadows. I heard metal against stone, a knife sharpening. My brothers filled the basin, first with water, then milk. My father reappeared and ran his hand through the mixture, nodding to say the temperature was good. The Russian told my brothers to leave, and with a confirming look from my father they did as he instructed.

"Perhaps you as well," the Russian said, upending a glass flask into the folds of a yellow handkerchief. My father's silence spoke for him. "For what I am to do," the Russian said, "I must be alone."

"But I don't understand."

"Only until the procedure is over," he said. "You must understand. For such a delicate operation, I need the utmost of concentration."

I looked to my father for help, but now the Russian had me in his hands: one drove the silk handkerchief into my mouth and nose, the other pushed hard from the back of my head. I could smell the chemicals in the folds of the fabric – so sharp and bitter. I snorted and fought to keep them away.

"Breathe," my father said. "Breathe, Petrus."

And then with an involuntary gulp I did – I brought a breath down into my lungs, watching now as my father left, pulling the door of the barn closed behind him.

The Russian smiled and leaned down to kiss my forehead. "We are alone," he said, and I nodded, as if I already knew what he had in mind.

He undressed me in haste, using all the care a hungry man might pay so much meat on a bone. He pulled my shirt up and yanked my trousers down, and then pulled one foot free and then the other. When he had me as he wanted, he held me back at arm's length to look at me before he began.

"Good," he said, seeing that I had kept the handkerchief over my mouth and nose and was now breathing freely from it on my own. "Breathe deeply, boy. You won't feel a thing."

He pulled me toward him, then, pulled me round so that my back was flush up against him, and while reaching down in front of me and grabbing me as a woman at the market might a bunch of grapes, he assured me this wouldn't take long, and that then we could see about "that other thing."

Of what followed, I do not remember the knife.

II.

When I awoke in the morning it was to the sound of splintering wood and my father's urgent curses. I lay in my parents' bed, not on one of the straw mattresses my brothers and I usually pulled onto the floor.

"That filthy Russian!" my father said, and he lifted one of his olive-branch chairs high over his head and smashed it down onto the floor. "That whore's child!"

At first I did not understand his blind rage, but then I looked to my lap and felt the dull pain that reminded of me what I had become. I lifted my eyes to my mother's. I wanted to know the Russian had fled in the night – to know that he had left my father without a son and made it so his leather pouch was without its silver coins. But my mother shushed me, did that and pressed a wet rag to my head. "It will be all right," she said.

I watched my father circle the table, breaking a second chair and then a third. I hardly even remembered dinner. Could the stranger really speak Portuguese and six other languages? Or was he fluent in only my own tongue and knew but a single word of the one he called his own? *Kastraty*. It had sounded foreign because of how his tongue had held it, but the word was all the same. He was a liar, I thought. The man told stories and wanted nothing more than to fill his belly and please his heart. He had left with a jingle in his pocket, off to grow rich from his lust again and again.

I sat higher in bed, remembering more, looking with desperation to my mother. She held my hand between hers; she patted it, reassuring me with a nod as she muttered a silent prayer.

"Pantaloun!" my father said, bringing down a final chair. "This is who I am!" And he danced over the splintered remains, his knees jumping as high as the middle of his chest. "I am that imbecile Pantaloun!"

"Shh!" my mother said at last. "Petrus is awake."

And here my father's legs fell straight. "Petrus?"

It pained me to hear my name like this: a question. But as I looked from him to my mother, I sensed it would be all right. The man had said I would sing for the tsar, so surely it would be so. "I will make you proud," I said, "and sing for the Glory of God. I will come back and see you both, as often as I can. Why else would this happen? I will sing for the tsar."

"Listen to your son," my mother said. "Listen to Petrus."

My father came toward us then, his smile growing larger as he did, though no more certain. "Of course you will," he said. "Each castrato is born to sing a song." He sat beside me on the bed and patted me no higher than the knee. "Each castrato."

✴

In the century before my birth, numerous conservatoires were established across my land to provide orphans with food, shelter and a general education. But near the time of my father's childhood, a good number of these began limiting enrollment to students worthy of musical instruction. The best of these were in Naples, and so it was there that the castrati went.

I did not have to go. I could have stayed in Norcia. When it was time to talk of marriage with the other fathers in the village, my father could have said I had a birth defect, or that I had been bitten by a wild pig. "He will not give you a grandchild," he could have said. "But he has a strong back and two willing hands. He can make a good husband." There are ways, I mean. But my father would not have it, just as he soon would not look me in the eye. And so at last when I could sit again like a man in the saddle, he tore me from my mother's arms and off we went to the great city in the south.

With castrati, the four Neapolitan conservatoires had a product to offer a sponsor in need of a singer at a funeral, mass or holy procession. There were also sacred plays to fill and private concerts that needed talent. "You will find many opportunities there," my father said, "more than we could offer you in Norcia. And they will give you a good home."

"Yes?" I asked.

"Your mother says they are no less charitable than the church, and that you will find others there like yourself. You will be happy."

My mother hadn't told me this. All morning she had only cried, until at last she pushed my twin toward me and told him to give me a hug goodbye, saying this might be the last he'd ever see me. I wish I could say my twin shed a tear and ran after my father's horse. But not all twins are close, and so when I turned in my saddle and looked for his approach, I saw only the shrinking image of my family's wooden house.

Our first morning in Naples, my father and I met with the *maestro di capella* of the *Conservatoire des Poveri di Gesu Cristo*. He was a massive man whose chin disappeared into the folds of his neck as he sat across from us at his desk and fixed his eyes upon me. I thought he was a giant, a giant who would eat me, but when he spoke it was with a voice so small and distant, I imagined him a mute who had swallowed a canary.

"You are a believer in the church?" he said. I nodded. "Devout?" Again I nodded. "Let me see your hands."

I looked to my father, who reached for them himself. I stepped to the maestro's desk then and held out my hands as instructed. They were black with dirt beneath the nails. The maestro looked at them for only a moment before falling back into his chair.

"And how did this happen?" he asked.

I looked to my hands, not sure how to answer.

"It was a pig," my father said.

"A wild pig?"

My father nodded. "A horrible day."

The maestro pursed his lips, then grunted. He stood and walked to a harpsichord set up near a window, sat before it and played a few notes. He looked at me as if to question why I had not followed. I went quickly to his side and warmed up as he performed a piece from a popular opera. I sang as I always did, with my heart in my lungs and my chin lifted to the Heavens, and when at last my voice fell back to the earth, I opened my eyes to see my father stepping toward us.

"Well?" he asked. "Is he not talented? Does he not have the voice of an angel?"

My father leaned in over the piano. The maestro looked away.

"But he is a castrato!" my father roared. "Castrato!" he said.

The maestro stood from the harpsichord and moved toward the window, blocking much of the light. "The conservatoire is poor," he said. "We pay for yesterday's meat with today's performances. There are many mouths to feed and only so many plates. It is how we survive. It is how we protect the orphans. And more than anything else, we must provide for the orphans."

My father pulled me out of the building by one hand. "We will try the *Conservatorie de Sant Onofrio.*"

This time we faced three maestros rather than one. "No," the first said at the end of my audition.

"Certainly not," added the second.

"You say he is castrato?" asked the third.

The afternoon proved no better. "A voice without promise," I was told at *Santa Maria di Loreto*, while the last maestro at the last conservatoire offered a verdict no different than the first: "There are too many mouths to feed. But perhaps if you paid his way? Say fifteen ducats a year? It is only the cost of the meat."

Late that afternoon, my father walked me down the covered aisle of a sprawling outdoor market, past wooden cages that housed squawking chickens and out beneath the light of day. The crowd was thick, moving in every direction at once. We broke through and found a fountain, in which Poseidon stood surrounded by four spitting dolphins.

My father sat me down and did not speak. I did as he did. I turned my face between my knees and betrayed nothing more than my exhaustion and a good sweat. A woman argued with one of the men selling chickens. "For that price," she said, "you'd better give me two!" The man shouted at her, reaching into his cage and pulling out a single bird. He dropped it in his hand by one leg and demanded she feel its plump flesh.

"Where will we go?" I asked.

"You need not worry."

"And what will I do?"

"You will sing."

"But the men – "

"You will sing!" My father's hand was quick – I did not see it until he had my jaw between his fingers and was forcing me to face him. "You were born to sing a song. Do you hear?" I nodded. "May God strike me dead if I am wrong. Dead," he said.

We returned to silence then, and I sat there imagining myself performing, some ten years older, dressed in gold and red feathers, a Roman warrior with his voice in the clouds. I saw the blue sky and white clouds of the painted background, heard the applause of the audience, felt the breeze of flowers thrown at my feet.

"Stay here," my father said. He stood and lifted my chin in his hand. "Don't move. Do you hear me? I will go and find us something to eat. Don't move until I come back."

I did as he said. I sat at the fountain and waited. I sat there as he returned to the bazaar and disappeared into the river of people. For an hour I sat there, and then two. I sat there as the sun fell and the moon rose and the sun came up again. I sat there as the crowd thinned out beneath the stars and the people returned with the morning's first trade. I sat there so hungry I thought I might fall, I sat there until I believed I had forgotten my own father's face – because how else to explain it? He had not found food? Yes, that was it. He had not found food and so he had not come back to betray his word. But he would soon, he would not leave me, and so I sat there, as he'd instructed, waiting.

At last I could do it no more, and with great shame I stood from the fountain and stopped the first woman who passed. She shook my hand from her elbow and told me I was a filthy beggar. I asked others: women, men, children. "Food?" I said. "Can I have food?" But they ignored me or cursed me, and disappeared down one of the bazaar's dark corridors. I tried for an hour or more, before I saw a head above all the others: the maestro from the *Conservatoire des Poveri di Gesu Cristo*, the first and the kindest we'd met.

He came in my direction, his progress around the fountain slow because he was moving against the flow of people. I spit on my hands and chewed at my nails, trying to push away the blackened dirt. Then I was moving forward to meet him and walking backwards when I saw he would not stop. "Please, sir," I said, "I have found myself castrato and can think of no other way. You will see I am very – "

But with a step quicker than I believed him capable of, he moved his massive body around me and slipped into the crowd, saying I should return to my father, it was with him that I belonged.

As he moved away, I allowed myself the thoughts I had been keeping at bay. My father had left me. He had ridden our horse from town, stopped at an inn for the night and ate, wiping the grease from his mouth. I would never see him again. This was my father.

I ran to the fountain and jumped onto its outer wall, looking into the distance for the maestro and shouting, "But I am an orphan! I have no father! Maestro!" I jumped into the water and struggled past the dolphins circling Poseidon and looked into the crowd on the other side. All I got for it was wet and a few curses. He too was gone. I couldn't see him.

That afternoon, a child ran back and forth through the bazaar. He wore a purple cassock covered by a white surplice and stopped near me to sing for a man and a woman. The couple gave him a coin, though his voice was no better than mine, and then the child ran away to sing for another. I approached and sang the same song. But while this child received another coin, I got nothing more than a narrowed look.

When we were left alone, the boy pushed me hard in the chest and told me to leave him alone. But where could I go? I was wanted here as much as any place else. So I did as my brothers once did to me. I pushed the boy and fought, quickly dropping the child with the force of my hands. I felt a rush of pride – all these years I'd been the one to fall, and now this. The feeling was short-lived, however, disappearing when a coin hit me in the chest.

A crowd had gathered to watch. Some cheered and others laughed, and then more coins were flying in, hitting me in the legs and landing around my sandaled feet. "Hit him again!" they said. "Fight!" The child I had beaten pushed up on his elbows, still dazed. I dropped to the ground to gather my winnings, ashamed each time I pinched another coin, as if my stomach were somehow attached to my fist. The boy rose and came at me then. I didn't hesitate. I flew into him with my knee, pinning him back against the ground. He shrank into himself and shielded his face, but as the crowd moved in around us, cheering me on with its wild calls, I did not do what he expected; instead of throwing more punches, I pulled the boy's surplice and cassock off over his head and ran away with the garments.

I didn't stop for several minutes, until after I'd turned down a quiet street and seen an old woman throw a bucket of dirtied water from her second-floor window. A few doors down from the circle of dirt she'd darkened, I turned into a recessed doorway, my chest still jumping from my run. I stripped out of my old clothes. When I was through, I left my old rags behind, and Petrus Augostino Benedetto, too.

That evening, I knocked at the door of the *Conservatoire des Poveri di Gesu Cristo* and asked to see the maestro. He came out with his hands clasped behind his back and stood before me in the street, his face stiff and disapproving.

"I told you to return to your father. The church would like to care for society's poor, but it cannot always do it. Go now."

"I can do this everyday," I said. I stood with the hem of the cassock held close to my belly, but here I pulled it out away from me to reveal a wealth of coins. They lay there silver and shiny against the purple fabric, like a puddle of moonlight. "The people said I could sing like an angel," I told him, dropping the hem of my cassock and allowing the coins to clatter onto the cobblestones at his feet. "I can do this everyday," I repeated.

A small smile appeared on the maestro's massive face. He motioned for my hands. I held them out for his inspection. They were clean, polished well and filed. He dropped my hands and turned his massive body slightly to one side, opening a path to the conservatoire's door.

"Hurry up to bed," he said. "We have a nine o'clock curfew."

III.

In the chapel the next morning, I stood before the two-hundred children living at the conservatoire and confessed to the crimes I had committed. Vincenzio, the thin-limbed boy I had beaten, accepted my words as he accepted the return of his clothing – stiffly and with coaching. Then, with a final look to the maestro, he retrieved from a bench another cassock and surplice and offered these to me. My outfit differed from his only in the addition of a black belt. There were seventeen others who wore this uniform. I sat with them in front.

The building that became my new home was c-shaped and three stories tall. Classrooms, rehearsal space and the cafeteria filled the floors that faced the street; two wings of dormitories stretched away from this, the boys overflowing on one side and the girls set loose in the other like ghosts.

I suffered at first from homesickness. I sent short letters back to Norcia that an older boy helped me write, but even if they did not rebuke my father (on the contrary, they were hopeful, announcing to my parents that it was all happening, just as it had been foretold) they did not inspire a response.

Several weeks after my arrival, another of the castrati, then sixteen and ready to leave the maestro's care, gave his debut in a local opera house. The notes he sang reached so high, were held so long, that no less than six ladies fainted before he bowed to our thundering applause. I was far from my father and his sheep now, and I knew I could sing nothing like this. But I was still young and my talents were not completely unlike those of the other castrati my age. For now it was enough that I could be fit into the wings of an angel and sent out to stand watch over the coffin of another child taken by the plague; enough that I could scrape clean my bowl in the cafeteria each night, knowing there'd more of the same the next day.

Us castrati were separated from the others and kept together in a small attic that rose like a bump from the top floor of the boys' dormitory. I became friends with the child in the bed next to mine, telling him at night that one day I would sing for the tsar, that all of this had been foretold. The child did not challenge my words, and when he learned of my old home, he spoke at length about the sausage he'd once tasted from there.

During winter, our close quarters kept us warmer than the others, while in the summer we benefited from a breeze that played between the windows at either end of our room. But if our accommodations were better, our daily instruction was more demanding. In the winter, we woke at six-thirty; in the summer, we were up as early as half past four, already singing. This was not so for the orphans on the floors below us. They could rise silently and dress in a sulk, or curse us – the children they came to hate – and the songs that woke them.

In the winter, because the governors feared our throats would freeze, we were given warm broths with tender bits of chicken and perhaps a raw egg, while the others ate lukewarm and meatless stews or porridges that turned to bricks of gelatin if you left them long enough alone. Maybe this was too much for the orphans to bear. Fights broke out between us in the stairwell and the hallways and in the courtyard where we played for an hour each day. Sometimes it took only a taunt to get us to raise our fists: *Non integri! Puttini castrati!* Other days there was more.

One afternoon the following spring, when we were all still anxious to run off the doldrums of winter, we kicked a ball around the hand-pump that delivered the conservatoire its water from a dusty spring. Two goals were drawn on opposite ends of the courtyard dirt, and soon my team was up 2-1. Immediately after our second goal, Vincenzio, the child I'd stolen from and left wearing only the smallest amount of wool, tackled me hard, reminding me how quickly he had grown. "We should call this game Castrato," he said, picking up the loose ball. "We kick around what they don't have."

Some castrati would ignore their tormentors or sing beautifully in the face of hazing. They were proud of who they were, and thought everyone should be jealous of their talent. Others ran away, including one eight-year-old who took off in the night that January, perhaps from a bad dream. We awoke to his screams and found the attic window pried open, and blood splattering the snow below. But I was unlike these castrati. I neither ran nor turned my back. I fought.

That day in the courtyard I flew into Vincenzio, screaming and flailing my limbs. Only he had grown thick where I had grown soft, and so for a moment he danced around me smiling, waiting for me to tire. Then he straightened his arm and dropped me with a single punch. But if he was to become a prodigy with his fists, I was already one with my chin. I rose, then fell once again. Five times in all he dropped me. But it was he who walked away. "Come back!" I screamed. "I'm not done!"

My good friend Giuseppe, the child who slept nearest me at night, was the first to approach me from a cluster of castrati. He placed his hands on my shoulders and looked me in the eye. "If you want to avoid this in the future," he said, "you must learn one thing."

I wiped the blood from my mouth, the tears now coming.

"Become a lover." He laughed and said it again, slapping me in the side. "A lover like me!"

If I loved one thing it was music, but it did not love me back. Would my father still be enchanted if he heard me coming through the hills? Had I ever been able to sing at all? The maestro had us perform before a mirror so that we could see those ugly contortions of the mouth and carriage that we needed to avoid. I tried to sing as long and high as the others. This left me doubled-over, my chest jumping for air. The maestro would look at me, and then his tiny canary's voice would appear. "Petrus," he would say. "Petrus." That was all, and then sometimes he would leave and Guiseppe would gladly say the rest. "The Diver!" he would shout. "This will be your stage name, Petrus – The Diver who comes up for air!"

He was my good friend, so I saw this for the fun that it was. But if he carried on too long, I would taunt him with musical theory, or ask if he could name all of the castrati back to Pietro Paolo Folignati and Girolamo Rosini. He couldn't, of course. He barely even knew they were the first to be entered into the register of the Papal Choir, while I knew them all.

At the end of our day, while my friends performed counterpoint or picked up a violin or other instrument, I often snuck downstairs to the larger rehearsal hall on the second floor. There, I'd stand outside the door with my back flat against the wall and listen to the noise coming from inside – the many harpsichords going at once, the violins attacking the same tune in different keys – and then at last I'd isolate the voices. A bass here, an alto there, all of it so unfamiliar, and then a tenor and a soprano, voices reaching for our heights but never getting near. Some of these singers were not so bad, though their talents would have been the subject of polite ridicule in our room. But I was not there to listen to them. I enjoyed hearing the others, the boys who could not sing at all. I'd close my eyes and smile, taking in their broken voices, their gasps for air, and I'd lose myself completely in it, just as I had once lost myself in a beautiful song.

By the time I was thirteen, I had noticed why the board of governors kept us away from the girls. We ate at separate times, and did not take our fresh air together. Still I looked for them everywhere, and when their singing came from a room in the other wing of the building, I'd go to my window and press my face to the glass and stare across the courtyard. Shadows and dreams, that's all I saw. The shutters were always closed, and if I caught a glimpse of them elsewhere, it was only while passing the laundry room, where they'd perspire over huge black cauldrons, pushing the clothes around with a tall wooden pole.

Then one afternoon, as if in payment for all my silent longing, I saw a girl standing on the third floor at her dormitory window. She stared into the clouds, and I knew she was alone because the other girls were singing on the floor below. I stood at the water pump in the courtyard, admiring the thick brown curls that hung over her shoulders and the long and slender curve of her neck. Then Vincenzio knocked me down from behind and shouted for me to get up and fight like a man.

It was rare that a month passed without our brawling, but as he kicked dirt in my face that day I could not summon the desire to respond. I kept trying to look at the girl. He kicked me, first in the legs, then the side, circling around and knocking me down each time I tried to rise. "Get up and fight!" he said. "Fight like a man!" I started to laugh. This infuriated him all the more. "I don't want to fight," I said. "There's a girl! Look!"

He pulled me to my feet, then, and spun me round holding my wrists together in one hand, grabbing the back of my head in the other. "What girl?" he asked, pushing me forward to the far wall, where a group of the conservatoire's youngest boys were gathered around a charcoal drawing of a donkey. "You're the only girl I see," he said, releasing me while pulling my cassock up over my head. The children parted as I was thrown into them, all but the blind-folded one holding the fox's tail. After hearing me land at his feet, he pulled the blind-fold off and saw me reaching to cover myself. Vincenzio shouted, "Here's a new game! You don't put the tail on the ass, you put it between his legs!"

It was the loudest laughter I'd heard yet, laughter I can still hear today. And when I recovered from it, and the maestro had emerged and Vincenzio had thrown my clothing back, the girl in the window was gone.

Her name was Alessandra Benedetta Calma, she was fourteen, and her mother had been murdered by her father. Calma. Alessandra's face was more frozen than calm, and like those who have come late to tragedy, it held a look of surprise or confusion.

"I will marry her," I said one night to Giuseppe, who sat up in bed with a laugh.

"You will marry? Is this before or after you will sing for the tsar?"

I stood at the window nodding. The sky was so thick with stars I expected the girls to appear sighing and sleepless from behind their shuttered windows. "Alessandra Benedetta Calma," I said. "She will be mine. I am sure of it."

Giuseppe laid back with his hands behind his head. "That is not the life for me. I will be too famous for only one woman. I will take the name 'Galterio' and sing for the Pope and the most powerful kings of Europe. I will have a different woman each night," he said, "and forget a different woman each day. 'Galterio.' Men will speak of me like a conquering army."

I turned to see his eyes lifted to the ceiling, lost in his fantasy. Already the maestro had said his voice was the clearest and strongest he'd heard in years, and certainly I did not doubt it – Guiseppe could carry a note longer than I could carry an egg on a spoon.

"My name will be Norcinelli," I told him, and here he laughed a second time.

"Oh, you are a fool indeed!"

"Why?"

"After a town known for more than just its sausage?"

"For my home and my father," I said.

"Your father?"

I looked from window to window, waiting for the first girl to appear. "You must respect your own father," I said.

"No matter what he has done?"

"No matter," I said.

"Then you are an even bigger fool than I already imagined," he said. "Least of all for believing you'll ever see the tsar."

"I will," I said, turning from the window and getting into bed. "I will sing for the tsar and the Glory of God. You don't believe me, but I will be the greatest singer Russia has ever known. It has all been foretold."

Giuseppe answered with fake snores. I waited until I was sure he was asleep, then I got out of my bed and dropped down to my knees. I said my prayers like always, but now with an urgent whisper. I didn't believe what I had told my friend. This was the problem. Weeks back, maybe months, I had begun to doubt it myself. But I still believed in something that I thought believed in me, and so I spoke to it because I had no one else.

Near the end of my fourteenth year, the maestro found me outside the main rehearsal hall, listening to the boys singing off-tune. He took me into his office and showed me to a seat in front of his desk.

"I want to tell you a story of a former student," he said, sitting at the bench before the harpsichord. "His name was Conti and he could sing like no other. When his father brought him to me, he said the child was born a natural castrato. This was a lie, of course – it always is. But what did I care? Whether you are bit by a pig or blessed by God, it makes no difference to me. I thought only of his talent, which I was sure would bring me great fame."

His fingers tapped out a short series of notes. "He absorbed everything, my Conti. He was a wonder to teach and a wonder on stage, so beautiful and poised. A marvel, really. But on the night of his debut, when already there were rumors he'd join an opera house in Rome, if not the Papal Choir, well, perhaps he held the note too long, for what had been harbored inside his body all these years now dropped between his legs. Does this make sense to you? He may have been a natural castrato, but no more. When his manhood dropped, so too did his voice."

The maestro stood and crossed to the window. "You might as well have torn up the floorboards – it would have been no less an interruption. He tried to continue – bravely, he did, but Conti no longer even knew how to stand upon the stage, and so by the time the last broken notes had fallen, the scouts for all the opera houses were gone, and with them his contract too."

He turned back from the window and came over to his desk. "I comforted him the best I could. I let him return here and for a time we believed he might make a living as a tenor. Sometimes, when he got drunk, he would even make a show of things and pretend to be a bass. But singing is not all in the voice, and something in Conti was different. He looked ugly on stage, slow and unsteady. I wasn't the only one who couldn't watch. He left one night without telling us. I was glad to wake the next morning and learn he was gone.

"I didn't see him again until last year, when I was traveling north near Milan." The maestro sat in his chair and only now began to look at me. "Conti had found a position in a provincial church choir, and so there he sang, fat and unshaven, with his wife and three children sitting in the pews, each of them a blessing as unexpected as the lumps between his legs."

He shook his head at the memory. "It was a damp and ugly hall. I could barely stand to stay. But I did, if only to speak with him afterward. He said he was happy, but he looked no different than anyone else who says this. I told him I was happy for him, too, and we left it at that. I don't imagine I'll see him again."

The maestro was now finished, but I did not dare speak a word. I only made my discomfort known by looking up from my lap and glancing in his direction.

"You are thinking," the maestro said, "of what happens to a castrato who cannot sing."

I kept my eyes on him. I had been thinking just that.

"This is why you listen to those boys who cannot hold a note. It's good to know your limits. But there is still a future for you. You can join a school," he said, "and teach others. You know a great deal, more from books than all the others combined."

My voice cracked as I spoke. "But my father said every castrato is born to sing a song."

The maestro smiled politely. "We cannot keep you here forever."

I started to understand. I was approaching Conti's age. "But I am not even fifteen."

"As is Giuseppe. And already I have secured for him the opera house and advertised his debut."

I had not heard. "And me?"

"You can pray he will be offered a contract and achieve some level of fame."

"But when will I have my debut?"

He rose from his chair and came around to sit on the near corner of his desk.

"I had thought we could train you for a life in the church, but while your heart is open, your fists are too often closed."

"But my name is Norcinelli. I will sing on the Russian stage. For the tsar."

"You cannot hold onto this."

"It has been foretold," I said. "You must understand, maestro. This is God's will."

He laughed. "And what was God's will for Conti? For him to be born a natural castrato, or for him to hit a note so high his next note came out so low? Because if it is the former, how do you explain the latter? And if it is the latter, then God can only be a madman. And if it is neither the former nor the latter, but a combination of God's will and the powers of Conti's voice that dropped his manhood between his legs," he swatted the air, no longer even looking at me, "then I do not know what to think – it is too complicated – we would have to go through life like men preparing to build a bridge – everything would be a measurement, and what kind of life is that? God's will," he said. "No, don't speak to me of that. It lays hidden from us and then one night drops down between your legs to take away your certainty."

I held my hands in my lap. "You are asking that I not believe in God?"

"I am saying, if you wish to make a life in music, you should practice more on the harpsichord."

I looked up.

"I have made a life for myself," he said. "You can do the same."

"Maestro?"

He nodded. "I am no different than you."

IV.

On the night of his debut, Giuseppe's voice was as full as the August heat. He revealed it gradually. He was like a dancer faced with a flight of stairs. He did not want to race to the top. He wanted to call your attention to every step. I stood in the back of the opera hall, breathing the stale, thick air. My friend was wonderful, but I felt the punch of something beyond his voice, something hard and impenetrable that had remained elusive all these years, like when the maestro took us to Vesuvius to sing into the crags and hollows of the mountain to check for imperfections in the echoes of our voice. My parents had left me, and since then not sent a word. I could not go back to them, but I also could not stay. I hated the harpsichord. I had prayed every night, and for what? It was no use. I felt as if I were shouting down an empty hall.

The maestro sat in a box overlooking the stage. He was joined by two men and a woman, the last of whom sat with flushed cheeks and bated breath, her bosom trapped high in her blue dress. I wanted to know the comforts she could offer. Her, anyone – it didn't matter. But while the Russian had been right to say we were capable and acquired the same urges as any man, he had failed to mention that we remained in one important respect a boy. I dared not show myself to a woman.

I rose from my seat and struggled down my row, then fled through the exits and pushed out onto the street, chased by Giuseppe's high, pure voice. A full moon hung in the sky, and no sooner had I looked up to it than I bumped into a wall of flesh – a woman stepping from a doorway with her scarlet dress pulled high to show the night's silver light playing out against her thigh. She stood close and breathed warm words into my ear. Then her hand moved down beneath my belt and cupped me where I had last been felt by the Russian. She quoted her price, her hand continuing now, slowly, as if in search of something she'd misplaced, until she laughed, realizing the mistake. "For you," she cried, and I was already running away, "a special price! Come back! It's all right! I'd like to try!"

I did not stop until I had found the conservatoire's steps and turned into the stairwell, where, on the landing between the second and third floors, in a corner given light by a window framing the moon, I came upon Vincenzio and Alessandra, the one turning to look at me square-on, the other quick to push her dress down and throw her hands up before her face.

"Get out of here, you fool!"

Vincenzio spoke these words to me, but it was Alessandra who heeded them. She pushed herself free and hurried up the stairs, leaving Vincenzio to trip over his pants – they were around his ankles – as he gave chase. A door slammed between them. Vincenzio stood, pulling his pants to his waist, and turned to face me. He descended slowly, with his face set. Then his fist rushed forward out of the dark and I fell.

I came to alone, tasting my own blood. Upstairs in our room, all the beds were made; the others were still at the performance. I changed into my night clothes, not even bothering to open the window to release the trapped heat, then got down on my knees to pray. I tried, but I could not whisper my usual thanks for the day. The room was too large and too quiet. I was not used to such silence. So at last I lay down and prayed while under the covers and staring up at the ceiling.

"Appear to me," I said, fearing something blasphemous. I told Him I still believed, but that I needed to know why I had been made like this. "Just please appear to me," I said. And then Giuseppe stormed in drunk on champagne and declared he would no longer be known by any name but Galterio, for he had been reborn – he sang a soaring note – and this was a new world in which everything would be his own. "I am Galterio!" he repeated, as the others rushed in around him. "Now bring me your women!"

I lay there, my prayers interrupted, and pretended to be asleep.

Some say what controls a castrato's growth is that which is taken from us. Perhaps this is true, for we rise to rare heights. Giuseppe was close to two meters when he left, and his chest looked no different than mine, having expanded to the size of a barrel. Measure me from side to side, I tell visitors to the tsar's dream city of St. Petersburg, and you will see it is the same measurement as you get from front to back.

But the capacity of the lungs bears only as much influence on the music captured therein as the walls of a wine barrel dictate the quality of their contents. In the weeks following my friend's departure, I emptied my lungs again and again for the maestro, trying to prove him wrong and sing a beautiful song. I stood before the mirror day after day, my feet held close together, my back straight, my chin tilted just so. But it was volume he said he heard, not music. I tried to sing harder and louder. I thought if my voice found one more note, held it one beat longer, I would emerge onto a new plateau. But before I could get there, I would double over before the mirror, gaping like a caught fish.

One afternoon, I stayed at my harpsichord instead of going to the mirror to sing. I wanted the maestro to tell me there was still a way, that I shouldn't give up, and that he was only pushing me so I might succeed. But instead he appeared at my side and said, "Good. It's sounding better. Continue." As he walked out the door, I played as if chopping carrots. The notes came out quick and uneven, until at last, like a knife sweeping a pile of cuttings to one side, I pulled my fingers across the keys.

That night, the maestro came up to our room with a new child, whom he left to our care. He was Giuseppe's replacement, and though there were two empty beds in the room, I told the newcomer to take the one farthest from me. He did not argue. I was the oldest, and he already knew I would soon be parted from my mattress and my sheets.

Mornings that fall, I lay half-asleep longer than the others, cursing their cheery diligence like the boys on the floors below. *Laudate, Pueri Dominum.* Children, Praise the Lord. Again and again. I'd perform my morning chores silently, not even bothering to move my lips along to the words, and only over breakfast would I occasionally forget my troubles – and then only because others had troubles larger than my own.

Alessandra had become the subject of rumors. I saw her often, having learned her schedule as best I could. But when she was let out into the courtyard each morning with the other girls, or when it stormed and she'd lean out her window to open her mouth and catch the rain, I could not see what had been suggested.

One day in the courtyard I was rolling marbles, crouched with my back to a cluster of boys, when I looked over my shoulder to see it was Vincenzio talking about her.

"She'll be gone as soon as the governors learn of it," he said.

"And the father, if he's discovered?"

"Gone as well," said another boy.

"Not if it's one of our teachers," Vincenzio cracked, and there was a good deal of laughter at this. Yes, everyone agreed, then the girl would be removed, but not the man. "It's a shame," Vincenzio said, "she's such a pretty girl. But then I guess it's the prettiest ones who are most vulnerable to such accidents."

I clutched a marble tight in my hand and turned round to face them. "You say this was an accident?"

My words were hard and confrontational, but Vincenzio's face softened when he saw they'd only been spoken by me.

"It was no accident," I said. "You know that."

"I do? Then what was it? Tell me."

I wanted nothing less than to expose his role. But I felt just as strongly that we had better not fight. He'd beaten me several times already, but where once his hands had sufficed, now I feared that nothing less than a stone would do, or perhaps a knife. This is what life required: a progression, change. I dropped my marble and looked to where it fell.

"I only mean to say I do not believe in accidents."

Vincenzio clapped me on the cheek. "Then tell me, what did God mean for you when he sent the teeth of that wild pig between your legs?"

I did not answer. He did not touch me, did not even mess my hair before he walked away. The other castrati, they urged me to rejoin their game.

That evening at supper I sat across from the child who had taken the far bed in our room. He was an eight year-old from Brindisi whose black hair hung in thick clumps over his eyes. He would not look at me. He glanced left and right, but found the conversation on each side walled off by a turned shoulder or a firm back. I thought he must not want my company, but then I remembered my own silence and the many barking commands I'd given him since telling him to take the other bed. He and his father had arrived at the back door where we received our milk. He was scared and still alone.

I set my spoon down and leaned in over my bowl. "It will be all right," I said. "You will like it here. We all do." They were lies, I knew. But then I had been comforted by them as a child, and so it was only right that I now give what I had received. "The maestro is an excellent teacher, and very kind. You'll like it here. The food is not so wonderful, but you'll survive. God watches out for us. He has brought you here, hasn't he?"

The child nodded. I picked up my spoon and motioned to his soup. He ate. But before I could do the same there was a noise from the hall, a girl's voice, unfamiliar in its proximity and volume, and then a familiar face. "Did I make this baby myself?" The maestro, two governors, and a priest in a black robe surrounded her as she spoke. "That's all I ask. Is it another virgin birth?" The priest slapped her, the maestro grabbed her shoulders and leaned in close to deliver a hushed and urgent plea; the governors helped move her out the door.

We in the hall were silent until the door had closed behind them, then we rushed to the window to see. At the hand-pump in the middle of the courtyard, the governors turned Allesandra over to two young nuns, who pulled her away to the door in the fence that opened onto the street.

She didn't know my name, I realized. I'd never told her. The one woman I had loved, the one I was sure I would marry, and she was as much a stranger to me at the end as at the beginning. I did not know if God had brought her to me only to show me what I could not have, or if He had brought her to me and I had failed to act.

The child from Brindisi stood alongside me at the window when the others turned away. "It will be all right," he said.

And so I shrugged, and nodded, and together we returned to the table and ate.

In April, the last available bed, the one next to mine, was filled by a young child so precocious in song – or so he thought – that he promised not to forget us in his fame. "Would you like to be my servant?" he asked one night. "I will need someone to care for my wardrobe, and to apply my make-up for the stage."

"Go to sleep," I said, half-wishing another new child would appear to force me onto the street. "Go to sleep and be quiet."

That night, I prayed again as I had since Galterio's debut: in my bed, not on my knees, and with no greater purpose. "Dear God," I began, "appear to me so I might know. Give me a sign."

And it was then that I heard it.

"Come down here, you animal!"

I sat up in bed and swung my feet to the floor.

The voice spoke a second time. "Come on, you coward! Show your face!"

I rushed to the window and saw Alessandra standing at the red hand-pump, holding her bundled baby high. "You want her? I'll leave her right here. The blood will be on your hands!"

A boy yelled out his window: "I don't want her, but I'll take you!"

Laughter rose from the floor below us, and then a crowd of castrati pushed in around me at the window, the children asking who it was and what she wanted and what had happened to bring her to this. "Shh!" I told them. "Let me listen!"

"What kind of mother are you?" screamed a girl from the other side.

"If you're a man, Vincenzio, you'll come down here and take this!"

I grabbed my gown and shoes and went downstairs. "Claim your child!" I heard her cry through the window on the landing. Then I pushed through the door and moved out across the cold dirt of the courtyard with my shoes still in my hands.

"There's your man!" cried one of the orphans. It sounded like Vincenzio.

Alessandra pulled her baby closer when she noticed my approach. "Get away from me!"

"Forget Vincenzio," I said. "I can make it easier."

"It's you," she said.

I stood on one leg, putting on one shoe and then the other. "Be my wife," I said.

"What?"

"It will be easier, together. Be my wife."

"This is a proposal, then?"

"Let this child be mine. I'll be good to her and to you, and for this I only ask that you let me love you as I'd like to be loved."

The boys heckled from above, calling me castrato, *non-integri*. Alessandra stood silently, not answering me. Her eyes moved from mine only when a light appeared to our left, on a floor that stretched between the two wings of the building – the maestro's room.

"You're castrato?"

It came out like a question and a curse. I looked past her, to the small door at the end of the wooden fence that enclosed the courtyard. It opened out onto the alleyway behind the street. I nodded. "I no longer know my name, but I know that I am that."

"Well," and here she bounced the baby up onto her shoulder, "I suppose that means I'd better hold onto this."

V.

We were married near Milan, in the church where Conti, the unshaven castrato, still sang. He told me of another church in another quiet town, and for a while I sold my services there. But I made little money, and we did not feel the comfort of friends. Worse, I felt like an oddity, a castrato employed only for the facts of his body, not the richness of his song. So we moved, going from town to town and inn to inn, often relying on the kindness of strangers to keep us in clothing and fed. I was good with our child. Her name was Orianna. Soon Allesandra was good with me. "It's all right," she said, the first time she saw me in bed.

For five years we struggled, though the struggle became more routine. In Bavaria we put up posters, advertising performances of *The Great Norcinelli – three nights only!* and were pleased on the first evening to peek out from the curtains of a beer hall and see a full-house turned as often to the stage as they were toward the taps. The same was true in Vienna, though there too the second night was not as good as the first. And even in Mannheim we made enough money on day one to be happy with the fall-off on day two and tolerant of those who came on the third to throw vegetables and scream their drunken obscenities.

I was the like the greatest of the castrati. I made my own schedule and performed only when the desire struck. In between my times on stage, Allesandra and I lived in small towns, taking a bed in an inn that would allow us to stay longer if she helped with the cooking and the wash. By the time we reached Dresden, Orianna could walk and speak and even sing. The third night's performance was always better now. If the drunks began to replace my voice with their own, Allesandra would usher our daughter out onto the stage, where she would sing a simple song to the delight of the belching crowd. Coins would fall where tomatoes once had. Some nights she sang from my shoulders, sitting there with her hands buried in my hair. Others, she held my hands and stood, singing from a greater height.

Our finances improved. We began to save gold coins in a plain leather pouch I wore around my neck. Allesandra said we should find a small town on one of the great trading routes and there establish an inn. I didn't resist because I wanted to continue to sing; I feared only our not having enough money to start. So we continued on the road, going from beerhall to beerhall, until I found we were in Württemberg, that city that had supposedly robbed the Russian of his silver cross and left him without his coins. Allesandra said we should travel through; she knew the story now and didn't feel it was right to stop. But I insisted, and so the cart that had given us passage stopped long enough for me to hop off to receive my wife and child and bags.

Allesandra and I argued before we even reached the inn. "You go where joy takes you," she said, "not sorrow; you're a fool to have stopped." I told her I was not thinking of the past, it was simply a chance to perform, to make money and bring us closer to our dreams. But maybe she was right. Before I could ask at the beerhall if there was a stage I could hire for the next night, I found a stool and had a drink, and then another, and another. I was in the cups by early evening, and swerving out the door at an hour I cannot name. I awoke in the mud the next morning, and sat up squinting into the sun. It took just a second for me to realize it. I reached for my neck; the pouch was gone.

What had happened? I had only shattered memories of what came between then and now. Highwaymen: that much I knew. But Allesandra didn't want to hear this. When I arrived at the inn, she was downstairs in the kitchen, serving a bowl of warmed oats to our daughter. She set one out for me without talking. I tried to explain, but even on the next wagon out of town, she said she didn't need to hear.

In the coming months, I sang worse than ever, and so we limited our engagements to two nights and kept to the smaller towns. Then we reached Berlin and I had an idea – we would return to Naples and I would see if the maestro would give me work teaching what I could not do. My wife agreed to this, and so to pay for our passage south we rented one of the better music halls and pasted posters all over town advertising a single performance: *See Norcinelli! The famous Italian castrato trained in Naples alongside the Mighty Galterio!*

What follows is either proof of God's will or evidence of the atheist's crutch, luck. All I can share are the facts: a messenger came to me backstage in Berlin, saying the tsar was sorry he could not see my performance, but perhaps he could enjoy my company later that same night.

"He is staying in a lodge in a wood to the east of the city," the messenger said. "My wagon will take you when you are done."

I looked to my wife and daughter, and then to the red curtain behind them. Beyond it, the crowd stamped its feet, whistled, called for the show to begin. All the seats had sold; the money was more than enough to return south, but this new idea I could not resist.

So I said that while I was honored to have received the interest of the tsar, I could not perform freely.

The messenger spoke capable French and passable German. He said perhaps he should not be saying this, but he believed it not one performance the tsar required, but a prolonged engagement.

"You will be adequately compensated," he said, "of this I can assure you. Now," he raised one hand and turned towards the stage, "I will wait for the end of your performance, and then" – but I grabbed his hand before it fell and dragged him towards the door.

"You have impeccable timing," I said. "The manager was due to announce the cancellation at any moment. If you had come five minutes later, we would have already been gone. You see, the room we have in town," and I glanced over my shoulder to make sure my wife and daughter were following me to the man's carriage, "there was a terrible draft last night. The milk and honey I have been drinking has yet to take effect. But now at least we can arrange my next performance with the tsar. Impeccable timing," I said again, handing the man his whip.

He nodded slowly and stepped up to his seat. Moments later the horses were off at a trot, and I sat smiling across from my wife and daughter, taking leave of Berlin before the crowd's first impatient boos.

The tsar sat on a stuffed divan, drinking tea served by a French giant who crouched before a fire, poking at the flaming logs.

"His name is Bourgeois," the tsar said in a German better than my own. "I found him last year in Calais." I looked to the man while drinking my own cup of tea. He was several centimeters taller than the tsar, who in turn was only slightly taller than me. "To the normal man," the tsar continued, "he is very much a giant, a fine specimen indeed."

The tsar refocused his attention on me. I shifted in my embroidered chair, uncomfortable despite the soft padding.

"I'm told you are ill?" he said.

"I'm sorry, yes. My voice, it's a cold. But soon to go away."

"Well, it will be all the more exciting then to advertise your debut in Petersburg. You have been told of what I am seeking?"

"A prolonged engagement?"

"Precisely. You will sing for my church and bed chamber," he said, leaning forward and glancing back to the giant. "His salary is quite handsome, you should know. Three hundred rubles. And yours will be the same."

I had to stifle a laugh. "Wonderful."

The tsar spoke as if not having noticed. "We will leave the morning after next, once I've had my shot at the local pigs. I expect you will be ready? I am to visit Tartary soon, and I would like to bring you with me to entertain The Khan."

After all these years, I thought, to sing for the Russian tsar!

"I assure you," he said, perhaps fearing my silence a negotiation, "if three hundred rubles is not sufficient," he glanced again at his servant, "I mean to say, I understand you are not merely an oddity of size, but a person of cultivated talents, of the arts. You will be richly rewarded, I promise."

I apologized for my muteness, hoping to appeal now to his superstitious side. "You must understand, this is all rather strange. As a child, a traveler came to my family and said he needed to procure just this: a singer for the tsar. And now here you are, and so long after I stopped believing we would meet."

The tsar considered this with the start of a smile, as if trying to remember if he had sent this man himself. He nodded. "Well, you will be ready to leave?"

"The sooner the better," I said. "I have only my wife and child, and they are waiting for me in the next room."

The tsar frowned. "You have a child?"

I told him it wasn't what he thought, and that I remained exactly what he required. He allowed himself a short laugh. "It is a shame the people of Berlin will be unable to hear you sing."

On this at least we agreed. "A terrible shame."

If I fooled the tsar, he also fooled me. After discovering in Petersburg that I could not sing, at least not well enough for his bedchamber, he brought me to his newly opened Kunstkamera, what some called The Museum of Ethnography and Anthropology, and others described as his Cabinet of Oddities. The salary he offered was more than adequate, and so I allowed myself to be shown to my room, where visitors soon after could be sure to find The Castrato of St. Petersburg.

It is not so bad a life. I have the freedom to wander the halls and inspect my employer's many collectibles. There are more than two-thousand embryological and anatomical specimens, including embalmed body parts, stuffed babies left sleeping on beds of straw, and whole fetuses kept in jars of varying sizes. The tamer displays show stuffed animals and birds, or thousands of insects offered up for inspection on the end of a pin. In two cabinets you will find dried plants. In another room, more seashells than a beach. But my favorite wing of the building houses the books: fifty-thousand volumes in Russian, Slavonic, Latin, Greek, French and German. Taken with my native tongue, they represent the seven languages I now speak – more, I'm sure, than my childhood's lusty visitor.

After seven years here, I was joined by Bourgeois. A glass coffin holds his skeletal remains in the center of the circular room where I spend the greater portion of my days. The giant's heart can be found in a jar in a nearby cabinet, floating in a thick, blue liquid that keeps away the decay of death. Alongside it on a glass shelf is a white card that holds two words in Cyrillic: Abnormally large. I will receive the same treatment when it is my time, for it is what the tsar, who last winter succumbed to death himself, had wanted.

You may think it strange, but I do not wish to leave. My salary is more than sufficient, as I have said, allowing me to support my wife and a daughter who is now of an age where she is growing into a woman and thinking of a love of her own. In short, I am as happy as any of us can hope to be, for I have all of this and the chance to sing my song the way I believe I was born to sing it. Each day I write.

In recent weeks, it has been my habit to compose my thoughts throughout the morning and afternoon at a desk set up for me at the far side of my room. On occasion, a visitor will interrupt my work, and then it is my duty to rise and present the many peculiarities of my carriage. I lift my chin and speak to the absence of an Adam's apple, pat my hips and thighs, and say they are as soft as a woman's. Then I fill my lungs and expand my chest to its greatest size. "It is this vast storage of air that gives my voice its strength," I say. "It is this that allows us castrati to sing as magnificently as we do."

With no further introduction, I launch into a brief aria, letting my voice rise and flutter like a bird circling the room. My visitors share approving nods; the women smile and fan their faces. They are all so pleased to have experienced this. But the truth is, the Russians are not an opera-loving people; they have no great history of music to draw upon. Few of my guests can even name more than two of the four vocal ranges between bass and soprano, and so to impress them, as is all too common in this life, I need only be loud.

THE BIRDS OVER THE VILLAGE N.

"Birds cannot be punished, but people can."
– Edward Radzinsky, *Stalin*

1.

How were we to know what was happening? In Petrograd the streetcars stopped running. Buildings burned and the sound of cannons shook the air. But here in Village N., we did not have a streetcar, only the train that stopped once a week. And though we did possess a cannon, it lay rusting in the fields, right where Napoleon's troops had left it in retreat. Word of Revolution came late to us, I'm saying. We heard of it only in November, after the first of our soldiers had returned from the front.

It was cold that evening, and a small crowd of us had gathered close besides the tracks, our faces turned toward the red smudge sinking into the horizon. We smoked cigarettes and passed a bottle of *samogon* back and forth, while the women held baskets of *syrniki* and skewers of salted fish they'd offer to passengers on the arriving train. When at last that train did pull in, young Dima was the first to step off.

"He has issued a decree!" he said, after we'd asked the soldier to repeat his first hurried words. "Lenin has promised that we're each to have our own land! Do you hear?"

We did – all but Galya, that is – but even after we'd shouted the words into her shrunken ear, we looked around no less confused.

"Who is this Lenin?" Some of us had traveled the rails, but even those of us who had could only speak of seeing the tsar or Kerensky in the newsreels. "What has become of Kerensky?"

"Forget him," the soldier told us, as the train moved off toward the darkening skies. "His government has failed, and Lenin is a greater man besides. He wears no homburg, but a good peasant's cap, like Ivan Grigorevich."

Hearing this, Ivan Grigorevich looked up from the bottle in his hand. "We're to have our own land?" he said. He might have only then awoken from a dream.

"Lenin is a great man," young Dima repeated, stamping his feet against the cold. "He stands more than two meters tall, and is as broad of shoulder as Peter the Great."

Ivan Grigorevich looked between us with a tentative and unfamiliar smile, the wind whistling through the gap in his teeth. "My grandfather owned only one thing," he said, reaching inside his shirt for the small leather pouch that hung from his neck. He opened its mouth and poured the contents into one hand. "This dirt," he said, "was everything to him, and he only had it because his master never knew. But now Lenin" – and the word had already become a leaden thing; it dropped before us like an anvil, solid and true – "has said we're to have more than that?"

"We're to have our own land," repeated Dima, glad to have regained the crowd's attention. "We have only to go out and claim it."

Ivan Grigorevich clenched his dirt in one hand, the pouch in the other, and then he was off, leading us even then, striding off toward the fields of Lavretsky's estate.

2.

Not all of us were such good Soviets before we learned it was Soviets we had become. And when we learned Lenin had given us our land only so he could turn around and take away our harvests – well, it was no easier to be a good Soviet then. But throughout those early years, when still some people refused to turn over their fields to the state, Ivan Grigorevich spoke with great belief, and we listened, always we listened because he developed a silver tongue.

We gathered one night in Lavretsky's old dining hall and sat in chairs lined up before a long table. Many of us took turns pointing to the bright patches of paint on the walls, wondering aloud what works of art had once hung there; others remarked on the fine grain of wood and marveled at how the boards were not worn from use. Then at last the room was full and our friend and leader rose from his chair at the front of the room, lifting a sealed glass jar in one hand.

"My grandfather left me only one thing," he said. "This jar of dirt." He raised it and turned it this way and that for all to see. "But this was no more his to give than it was his master's. Forget the rumors you have heard. That land" – he pointed out the window – "is not yours."

We grumbled as he talked; we whispered and some of us cursed. But then at last he moved his finger away from the window and sent it out over all of us.

"That land is ours," he said. "Not mine or his or hers, but ours, do you hear? It belongs to the good Soviet people, and who among us would dare take that for himself?"

There were such people present that day. But they did not announce their identity to the crowd. Instead, they returned to the farms their families had tended for generations and tethered their animals more tightly in their sheds. They cursed us and the communal farms we were building, saying they would rather give us their blood than their land. Well, we let them. One by one we came, led always by Ivan Grigorevich's hoarse voice and outstretched hand. "There is the tight-fisted one!" he would say. "There is the *kulak* who will feed himself so you might starve!" And so we pointed our pistols or tightened our ropes, and many died as a result of this or were at the very least sent off with their wives and children on the back of a horse-drawn cart. You ask was this difficult? 'No.' This is what we say, and to a man on it we agree. These were simple tasks for simple times. The nobles were the first to disappear, and the rich after that. What was there to question? Nothing, at least for a time. But after we had rid ourselves of them, we did begin to speak the quietest of doubts. Just what makes a *kulak* anyway? We didn't know, but Ivan Grigorevich was our better still. "There are peasants who are extremely poor," he would say, "and those who are no poorer than you. But there are also peasants who are perhaps not poor enough, and it is to them that we go tonight."

3.

Lenin, as you know, did not live to see the fruit of his revolution; Stalin picked it early from the tree and began to eat. But all along Ivan Grigorevich led us into the future, and so we followed him and we believed.

As we cleared the land where Lavretsky's estate had once stood, we believed we'd soon see a factory that would give us all a little work. When the barracks went up to suggest this was not so, we were pleased to be told of the agricultural university that Moscow had designed for our children. And at last when we raised the fences around these barracks – well, we were disappointed to discover we stood on the wrong side of a camp we could not leave.

Ivan Grigorevich received each of us in his office to enter our name and birth date into a log book, then gave us each a number we were told we should never forget. Finally, he would look up and place something before us.

"Do you see what we have here?" he'd ask, and certainly we would – a small corked glass bottle filled with dry dirt.

"Before Lavretsky was hung from that tree," he'd say, pointing out the window, "my grandfather toiled in these same fields. He worked this land and coaxed a living from it, much as I'd like to see from you."

He would grab the bottle then and cross to a cabinet at the far end of the room, saying, as he locked it away, that he would make a present of this dirt to us – "as proof of your contribution to the great Soviet state" – whenever we had shown we were rehabilitated.

For the first few weeks, no one found anything strange about this. But there were hundreds of us here, soon more, many more, and the cabinet in which he placed the dirt was only so large. Some among us believed he kept in his office only those vials of dirt belonging to the newest arrivals; the rest, it was argued, were moved to a storage shed, from which they would be returned to their rightful owners at their point of release. But others thought you had to be a fool to believe something like this. "That cabinet in his office isn't even full," these men would say. "There is only one bottle of dirt, the same for us all. He shows it again and again."

We argued about this fitfully, until at last Ivan Grigorevich came among us with an answer we didn't like.

4.

He was such a great man, we thought at first they had built a statue in his honor. That first morning we saw it, a thing of bronze that grew taller with each step, we only realized it was Stalin when we were close enough to stand in its shadow and marvel at the face.

"He will soon be here," one of the guards announced. "If not to spit on the likes of you, then to commemorate the opening of the canal."

With these words, we were sent to our work with shovels, picks, and some of us with only our hands. The canal was completed in August, and though we all had been told Stalin would appear with the first rush of water, the opening of the gates was accompanied by only a greater number of birds. The birds darkened the sun some afternoons, and as ours was an oblast with more open fields than trees, the birds often settled on our leaders's bronzed head, finding it the most suitable roost.

The morning he was told of the white streaks on Stalin's nose and cheeks, Ivan Grigorevich was not pleased. He led a small group of us from the camp, one man carrying a ladder, another a bucket, a third a broom, and all along he shook his head and muttered – it was the first we'd seen him so upset.

"Look at this," he said. For it was worse than he'd been told. Stalin appeared to be crying excrement. "If he sees this, do you know what will happen?" Being already in the camp, we knew too well. But still he explained, "Birds cannot be punished, only people can. Now clean!"

And so one man readied the ladder, allowing the next to go up with a bucket, and then another with a mop. In this way we made Stalin clean.

There were many birds that fall, more than usual, it's safe to say, so many in fact that those of us who were given the bucket or the mop or the ladder would often come back swearing there had been more shit than face.

Ivan Grigorevich for once looked more boy than man. Each week Moscow told him another thing. He's coming, he's not, he'll be late, he'll be early. "Get out there," he'd cry. "Clean it! What if Stalin comes in the night?"

One morning, before the sun was like a bloody egg wobbling on the horizon, Ivan Grigorevich didn't even wait for one of us to do the work – he went out there alone, smelling of *samogon* and pickles, and with a shotgun blasted at the birds in their sleep. When he sobered up enough to realize the danger of this act, he had a group of us roused from our bunks and sent us out with the ladder to make sure the statue stood unblemished. It did not, but the man who made the closest inspection, a painter of abstract anti-Soviet art, insisted that the damage done was actually an improvement. "The cheeks," he said, "they look pock-marked now. It's a remarkable resemblance to real life."

Even so, shotguns were not an option that could be deployed each day, and so the next morning at breakfast, a man was handed a bag of poison and told to follow the ladder out the front gates. That first day the poison was not very successful. Two birds fell dead by early afternoon, one over the camp, the other near the canal. The next morning, either all the birds were hungry or the man giving out the pellets gave out much more than he had the day before, because for an hour it was like a hard rain, with the birds coming down from the clear blue skies in thick black streaks, one after the other after the other.

If only Stalin had waited. If only he had come after we had determined the best way to kill these birds, then everything would have been different. But Stalin could be rescheduled no more easily than the seasons, and so one morning after we'd fed the birds but not yet been given reason to go out and collect them, a line of cars moved in from the distance on the long dirt road that stretched to the horizon.

Ivan Grigorevich met Stalin at his car and led him out the front gate to inspect his bronzed double. With a twitch in his eye and a hitch in his step, he looked again and again from the statue's face to the skies, more than once causing Stalin to stop and demand his full attention. It was a crisp and beautiful day, the first snow still a month or two away, the skies blue and thick with white clouds. The water ran through the canal in the distance, just as it had since the gates opened, and on it a single boat floated by. Stalin pulled up beneath his own shadow and lifted his hand to wave, mirroring the pose the sculptor had frozen overhead. The boatman tooted his horn in response and drifted to the south.

We prisoners were marched out and stood at attention in a group at Stalin's side, and even though we were where we were, some of us were no different than the guards: impressed, standing there with inflated chests and a mist in the eye, because it is rare that you are this close to history. Others were less taken by the man's appearance and whispered that this was not even the true Stalin, that it was only one of the Stalins the real man employed so he could be in every place at once, like that other dead revolutionary, God. But then all such whispered talk died, and the first crane fell from the Heavens with a bleating cry.

Ivan Grigorevich jumped forward as if propelled by a burst of air. He leaned in over the carcass and shook his head from side to side. Then the second crane fell like a sack of wheat at his rear, and the third turned him round once more.

We scattered like rats shown a slant of light, all of us throwing our faces toward the skies as the birds continued to circle and fall.

By the time it was over, Stalin was coming out from between the cover of his own legs, and we all knew that Ivan Grigorevich would be scratching himself among us in the barracks that night. It was true, too. He was there like many of us, there until he was gone, and though his mind wasn't as sharp at the end as it was in the beginning, he was always ready to reach for the pouch that had once hung from his neck and tell you a few words about dirt.

HUMBERT HUMBERT DOES UKRAINE

When women learn of the many stamps in my passport (eleven for Kiev-Borispol, thirteen between Moscow and St. Pete) they look at me as if I were an alcoholic unable to acknowledge what everyone else already knows. "Why?" they ask, and maybe they reach for my arm if we're sitting side-by-side at an airport bar. "Why go all that way for a wife?"

In the beginning, I didn't have a ready answer. Those first few trips, before I'd visited the Urals and Minsk, when I still mixed up Lithuania with Latvia and couldn't place Estonia on a map, I spoke of my first wife, or even less glowingly of the second. I said I was fifty-four years-old and looking for a little adventure, a man who'd been off the market so long he needed a little help. But then I wondered why I was saying anything at all. When a colleague of mine remarried, I didn't approach her after one of our committee meetings to say, "I see you went black this time. Any reason?" No, I didn't need to answer my interrogators, because they already had answers of their own. They had read the same newspaper articles and magazine profiles, had maybe seen a documentary or a segment on *60 Minutes*, and though they'd be loathe to suggest that all Mexicans or lesbians were alike, they'd be quick to agree that there could be only one type of man interested in a so-called mail-order bride.

"You want a woman to obey you, don't you? To cook and clean. To mother you in the kitchen and be your whore in bed. Or maybe it's not even a woman you're after. Is that it?" Where but at an airport bar does accusation come so easily between strangers? Let a woman in comfortable clogs and ridiculous gaucho pants hear her flight's boarding call and she'll reach for her carry-on and let loose with all that she's kept hidden before. "How old is she? Sixteen?" Her voice fell like a stone dropped into a well. *"Fourteen?"*

I sat there unmoving as she smiled down over me. I didn't dare lift my drink for the fear I'd reveal a shake. "What do you want me to say?" I asked when she was gone. "What are you supposed to say?"

I've told my story several times before, though until now it's been delivered in a piecemeal fashion. The man at JFK heard what the woman at LHO would never know, and the questions left unanswered at De Gaulle were given as non-sequiturs at Sheremetyevo. Realtors and Rotarians have sat with me on planes and in airport bars, as have German Christmas tree ornament salesmen and even a young woman from Edinburgh who claimed to make "post-feminist pornography" for a small but loyal band of web-cam subscribers. These are the holders of my biography, a book we might as well call *Humbert Humbert Does Ukraine* – isn't that what you'd prefer? And so to gather together all these loose fragments, to hear the truth, the whole truth, and nothing but the truth, so help me god, you'd only have to book tickets and make hotel reservations and put these many men and women up for the night at some SAS Radisson or far-flung Novotel.

Oh, to wear a fake mustache and false side-burns and fall in alongside them at the free breakfast buffet! As they spooned their congealed scrambled eggs onto their plates or pushed a button and waited for their instant cappuccinos, there'd be reminisces and laughter, and yes, moments when it'd only be appropriate to purse your lips and sadly shake your head. But come, they're moving now, off to the conference room where they'll take the podium one by one:

"He told me he went looking for a wife that first time, but he had so much fun he went back thinking it better to date. By his third trip, he had a serious case of Playboy-itis. He said, 'Gary, I have a serious case of Playboy-itis. Every time I leave Ukraine, I wonder why I'm going back.'"

"I just assumed he was a loser like all the rest. You know, couldn't find a date in America because he had a closetful of porno and a hundred dollar phone bill home to mother. Nothing special, just your average run-of-the-mill born-again teenager. Did I mention he had a mustache? Completely without irony."

"His second wife told him to hang a urinal in the garage. He worked in the yard on the weekends, and she was tired of him dragging dirt into the house. 'Can't you just buy a urinal?' she said. He told me he felt like a dog."

"But I will give him one thing: it takes a lot of courage to go halfway around the world to pick up some fox and drag her home with you. All that responsibility. My boyfriend keeps reminding me I can't even keep a goldfish alive. That mustache, though, my god."

"I don't know. Did he like them young?"

"That he didn't say."

"But you know he does. You just know it."

This would be a logistical nightmare, though, wouldn't it? What with so many conflicting schedules and all the various time zones to cross, you could never hope to pull off such a feat. No, to corral all the facts once and for all, it's better that I write this – too cutely perhaps, with screens and veils going up all around, but then if a man crosses an ocean to satisfy his most urgent desires, has he not earned – oh let me say it – the right to a fancy prose style?

For the Freudians and pop-psychologists among you, I offer the following:

I was born in London, in 1944, the product of an English mother, an American father, and Hitler's war. Following V-E Day, my dear daddy made a name for himself in coconut oil, allowing me to be sent away to school and boarded alongside His Royal Highness Prince Flick or Flack of Serbia and Montenegro. He was a cross-eyed toad, always running at the nose and pawing at his crotch, and though he was poorer than his title would lead you to believe (or more likely because of this) he kept a list in his diary charting his place in the line of succession to the British throne. Years later, when #87 married a Roman Catholic, my old roommate was stripped of his royal fantasies, as required by the Act of Settlement. "And it's funny," I wrote, in the card that accompanied the twelve-dollar toaster I sent to commemorate his nuptials, "you've been buggering boys all these years, and what do they get you for in the end? Sleeping with a woman who doesn't have the good sense to use birth control. Long live the Queen, and give my regards to the old woman on the throne as well."

After taking off my public school's blue and gold striped tie, I moved to America and one of the lesser ivies, from which I earned a Ph.D. in English Literature and found myself work at a private university west of the Hudson River that holds a nominal affiliation with the Methodist Church. Here I have remained, through bad presidencies and worse marriages and at last the death of my parents (they went within three days of each other, my mother going second with her usual lack of originality). But I shouldn't venture much further than this, as to do so would risk revealing myself too finely and tarring my employer with the shame of association.

Let me make myself perfectly clear: I confess to no crime other than the human sexual act. I just happen to do so at a time in our history when such behavior is considered criminal by many of my colleagues at Let's Not Be Named in a Lawsuit U. There was a time not so long ago when I could still walk the halls of this building and hear the squeaking of a love-seat behind an office door. It was a sound that made me want to kiss babies and uplift the poor. But now per university policy our doors are to remain ajar at all hours, and so the tenured medievalist sits alone on the third floor, not having published so much as a book review in years.

Are we the better for it? I wish you could see my students. They sit before me with the idiot-smiles of prolonged adolescence, wanting nothing more than to be told exactly what they need to know. The leaders of tomorrow's fascism, they are such a well-behaved group, sitting there quietly and attentively even during orientation week. Grab a hand-out on date rape, a bookmark for the suicide prevention line, and take a seat inside Wealthy Benefactor Hall, where, up on the screen, rising like the shadow of Nosferatu, is our annual sexual harassment awareness film. Do not blink. Do not ask to be excused to the bathroom. Buckle up and take it in. There is no joy left in Mudville.

I should have gone gay, even if only secretly like so many of my old classmates. Where else but among the former perversions is the sex act still viewed as something other than the demon seed? Promiscuity for them is empowerment; glory holes and slow walks beneath shaded bridges a cultural right. It boggles the mind, really. Consider the woman on the sidelines of the gay pride parade. See her wearing a pink feather boa as a show of support. Hear her whistle as the men parade past in bondage chokers and full leather chaps.

How enlightened she is! How free! She claps when men with full mustaches simulate sex acts while dressed as nuns, and she shouts you down as a bigot if you say this is filth or obscene. But meet her again on Monday morning and don't dare mention anything approaching the union of the cunt and the cock, because like her fellow employees she has initialed here and signed there and acknowledged the policy that prohibits unwanted sexual innuendo in the workplace.

"But how can you know if it's unwanted if it's not yet said?"

"You know what it means. Just sign the paper."

"But are we not literature professors? Do we not parse out the words?"

"He's only doing this because he screws his students."

"Am I supposed to just stand here while she says that?"

"Sign the paper, David."

"Isn't anyone going to say anything?"

"Close reading's been out of fashion since the sixties. You know that, David."

Tell me: Where is the place for it anymore? If not at work or the gym, if not in the church we've given to the poor and hopeless or the public square that fills no more, just where can we ever hope to meet someone to have sex anymore? On the back of a flat-bed truck driving 12 miles per hour through the streets of West Hollywood? At the Stonewall Inn? Yes, I should have gone gay. But there comes a time in a man's life when he understands on which side of a dick he belongs, and this side, for better or worse, in sickness and in health, appears to be mine.

To refocus:

Ukraine is located in Eastern Europe, around the latitude of nine degrees north and the longitude of 32 degrees east. It borders the Black Sea to the south, Russia to the east, and the countries of Moldova, Romania, Hungary, Poland, and Belarus to the west and north-west. The weather is for the most part temperate continental, though on the southern Crimean coast it more closely resembles the Mediterranean (without, it should be noted, too many Serbs or Montenegrins, which is just fine by me).

When I landed at Kiev Borispol on 4 June 1998 and descended the steps to the tarmac, it was 14 degrees Centigrade, with a wind coming from the north at seven miles per hour. The skies were mostly clear, the humidity high, and the women, including the mini-skirted hostess who waved me in toward the waiting shuttle bus with a gloved hand, exceedingly beautiful.

I stayed twenty-one days, paying $5,995 for a package tour that took me on to Moscow and through St. Petersburg, with nine champagne socials along the way. At these functions, where the women outnumbered the men no less than 5 to 1, I was joined by thirty-plus others, one man French, another Dutch, three Canadians, and the rest my compatriots from these Dissatisfied United States.

After settling into our hotel that first day, a group of us gathered in the room our tour organizer had set up as a temporary office on the third floor. We sat on love seats around a wooden coffee table and reached for albums that included profiles of all the women we could arrange to meet. When someone was done with A-D, he swapped out that album with the man who had E-H, etc., etc.,. For more than an hour we continued like this, studying photos and measurements and writing down the names and numbers of the likeliest candidates.

(Treating them like cattle, weren't we? Well, you're right. But tell me: where do you believe your Darwin and where do you pick up the Book of Common Prayer? Let your skirt fall to the floor; take off your boxer shorts and stand naked before the mirror. Men and women both, understand this: we are animals. Get down on all fours if it helps. Study your reflection. Say it aloud. Animal. Now, can we proceed?)

At the first social, I briefly shadowed a man who sat down before each of his prospective dates and flipped through pictures of jet skis, sky-diving trips, and his Harley Davidson motorcycle. He'd pause lovingly over photos of his sprawling ranch house in Denton, Texas, and speak softly while running his fingers across a photo that showed the dairy section of his local Piggy Wiggly supermarket. "Are you interested in this?" he'd say. "And what about this?" "But would you ever consider this?"

It didn't surprise me that these women had never thrown themselves out of a plane recreationally; certain pleasures are limited to the most advanced and wealthy nations. But it did surprise me to learn that so few of these women wanted to leave Ukraine. They outnumbered us seven or eight to one that night, and I'd venture to say that nine of every ten had only come for the free drinks, the dancing, or to meet a foreigner who'd be good for one date and a $20 dinner in a country where the average salary was still $150 a month.

Mr. Photo Album worked with a commendable efficiency. At the second or third "No, I'm not interested in that," he'd close his book and waddle over to the next table, his belt hidden beneath his aqueous belly. He tolerated me at first because our situation required good humor and mutual support, but shortly after I joked he would have made a fine U.S. diplomat, he rose and left me bookended by two Natashas, each of whom wore a dress that brought to mind Soviet wallpaper.

Our interpreter sat across from us in one of two unfixed chairs. She filtered her compatriots' questions and gave me their responses to my answers, and when the women learned I was a university professor, they clung to me as if I were a railing on a storm-tossed ship. I told them the attention was unwarranted, as no more than twelve people had read my most recent book – copies of which, I was quick to add, could be had for $1.99 on eBay. "Slightly more if it bears an inscription to a 'dear colleague' or 'my good, good friend.'" This only drew the ladies closer; they spoke of the coarsening fabric of the world and made me promise to let them feed me borsch. Then two others arrived, these no less matronly in appearance and no more uniquely named. "Anyas, you say?" What a laugh we had when I asked everyone to switch seats, if only so the two Natashas could sit on my left and the two Anyas on my right. Did it matter that I felt no attraction to any of them? Of course not. I sat there like a minor official of a major sultanate, a rare and intoxicating feeling indeed for a member of the Shakespeare Society of America.

But the women were not necessarily mine for the taking. I could not simply point and click my mouse and expect one to be shipped to my home in a cardboard box filled with styrofoam peanuts. I was reminded of as much when a woman came over from the dance-floor, younger than the others by about five or ten years, and took the empty seat by the interpreter. After lighting a cigarette, she sent a cursory glance in my direction – I wore a name-tag over my heart – and then looked back toward the crowd beneath the disco lights, allowing my gaze to more freely fall upon her. She had short red hair, piercing green eyes, and a sticker high on one shoulder that read "Hello, My Name is Olga." I had seen her in the folder marked P-Z and written down her age (27) and profile number (3X21L). But prior to my arrival, she had visited the tour organizer's office downtown and flipped through another album with photos and information on all the incoming men. Age. Location. Profession.

"You seem like a nice man," she told me in remarkably good English, "but I want to live in California, Hawaii or Florida" – she looked again at my name tag – "and I don't think you're on my list."

I went to bed alone that night, feeling like Churchill during the Battle of Britain: discouraged, and yet invigorated and full of purpose. While waiting for sleep to slow my thinking, I heard televised pornography through the wall from the next room, and when that shut off, a man crying in rising sobs and bursts. It was Peter from St. Paul, Minnesota, a tractor salesman and also the youngest among us at thirty-four. He had corresponded daily for five months with a woman from Chernigov who was supposed to have arrived that day on the afternoon train. When he'd come back alone to the hotel in the evening, ashamed to admit he had wired her the money for the ticket, we'd urged him to forget it and come along with us to the party. But he had a ring in his pocket, and so he'd opted to spend the evening in an Internet cafe, writing her a letter to ask if it was a mistake and she'd only missed the train.

I listened to him cry for a minute; then I pounded on the wall and we went to sleep.

My second trip to the Former Soviet Union was less than three months after the first. I remember a group of us sat at a sidewalk cafe on Kreshatik, drinking beer as good as any in Germany and for a fraction of the price. The economy was a shambles. Even here in Kiev's city center, Ukrainians relied on the crooked carrots and soft potatoes grown for them by relatives in the outlying villages. A corporate attorney from Atlanta was with us that day. He whistled and waved to a passing fancy, some long-legged girl in a leopard print dress who walked over with a smile to ask us where we were from. My travels to Ukraine have worked on me like yoga or meditation or years of intensive therapy. I tried next. I raised my hand when I saw something pleasing to my eye, then snapped my fingers and waved to get her attention. Unlike the first, she didn't speak any English, but she understood the power of the passport I showed to her. "American," I said. "I am an American."

I had sex with her and one other woman that trip, and yet if this were a score on the SAT good enough to get me into Cleveland State University on a partial scholarship, there were many other men I knew going to Harvard, including a corporate pig farmer from Fresno, California who considered himself a failure if his average fell to anything lower than one unique screw per day.

On the final afternoon of that trip, I sat next to a man in the hotel bar who was filling out four separate fiancee visas and considering the cost-to-benefit ratio of a fifth. "Invite as many as you can," he advised me. "You throw enough shit on the wall, something's bound to stick."

I stopped listening to him at some point, for as he spoke a young woman walked across the marble floor of the hotel lobby and inspired in me feelings of such uncommon strength and emotion that I must have gaped like a insensate monkey for five, ten, fifteen seconds or more. She was a young thing so beautiful you would have thought she had dripped out of Nabokov's leaky fountain pen. Pink heels, a short polka-dotted skirt buffeted by a layer of crinoline, and with her luxurious, brown hair done up in pig-tails and tied with pink ribbons. I never saw her face, but she did to me what I'd thought for a time only Viagra could. I rose as she neared the revolving door, not sure if she was sixteen or twenty-four or well on into her thirties. I'll never know either. I knocked into a barstool on my way out, stopped to right it and apologize, then pushed out onto the street, squinting against the bright light in both directions. She was gone, but a thought inspired by her remained. Perhaps she was a whore, someone who sat on the edge of the fountain in the park, opening her legs to show a passing foreigner that she wore no panties. Perhaps she was a sixteen year-old whore and there was another like her that could make me feel the same way.

If this was my most fundamental desire, had it always been or was it only because I came here and discovered it? Are we what we are, or are we always what we are becoming?

Four months later I was back again.

By the turn of the millennium, it wasn't just professionals and cashed-out dot-com'ers who were mingling with me in Eastern Europe. Now even plumbers and garbage men were chasing tabloid stories of sex for the taking. Unlike me, they wanted to come here but one time and spend no more on a new wife than they would a used car. I stopped going on romance tours to avoid these crowds and would hire a young local man wherever I went to serve as my driver and interpreter.

Nowhere was I better served than in Kharkov, a glorious city of stone architecture near the Ukraine-Russian border. There, my interpreter, Andrei, a young philology student at the city's oldest university, had me show up at the Metropole at ten a.m. one Saturday, so that on the hour for the next ten hours I could be introduced to a young woman who invariably turned in off Sumskaya Street and walked up toward my table in towering high heels. Andrei flipped through my photos, describing my interests and plans, my profession and home, and even perfected the delivery of some of my less complicated jokes.

I came close with one of these women. We spoke on the phone when I returned to the States; we kept in contact daily via email. It was like any other relationship, only we did things in a more concentrated manner. Instead of a courtship that saw us dating on the weekends over six months or a year, I came for three or four weeks at a time and saw her without interruption. When I returned to her a third time, I did so with a ring in my pocket. On what was to have been the second to last day of my stay in Kharkov, my girlfriend showed up at the door of my rented flat in the sort of knee-high boots I've found American women will most commonly wear for Halloween or while role-playing. Above these, she wore a fur held close together beneath her chin. A flash showed me why: she had nothing on beneath it but hip-bones so sharp they could have cut the ribbon on the new gender studies building at Wellesley College.

I should have proposed to her and been done with it, but I felt like the man at the blackjack table who's already won several thousand dollars: he figures he can press on and win more. So the following afternoon, I took a cab to the train station and left for Kiev a day early. That night, I checked into the Boryspil International Hotel and while listening to the planes take off and land, I thought of my little Lolita in the lobby of the hotel, the one who'd sent me tumbling into a barstool. Could she have been no more than fourteen?

An investment banker put it to me bluntly while we waited out a delay at O'Hare earlier this year. "Can you fuck the young ones? C'mon, you can tell me. You haven't even given me your name yet. You're flying east, I'm going west. What's it really like? Could I go there and fuck the young ones?"

We were drinking scotch and not eating enough, our voices whispers beneath the roar of televised football and those who were pushing in around us to watch. I stared down at the ice cubes in my glass, shrugged, shook my head, then looked up smiling weakly. What are you supposed to say when a man suggests you might be flying seven-thousand miles from home to bang a girl who still keeps her baby teeth in a felt-lined jewelry box by her bed? Did he think this could be easily arranged? That you could find yourself standing in the middle of a verdant green pasture in the poorest country in Europe, negotiating with an old Moldovan man for visiting rights to his daughter? Could he possibly imagine that the cost of this is only two milk cows and a pig? What would he have said if I told him the truth?

In the past, I'd fended off such talk with hasty rejoinders. "It's not about screwing young girls," I'd said. "It's about family values and finding a woman who still believes in 'till death do us part.'" I'd parried these questioners with statistics to hold up mirrors to their suspicions and doubts. "Four of every ten American women born in the seventies will divorce." "One in every three American marriages will end in legal fees." "That's why I'm going over there. To get onto a new actuarial chart." It got to a point where I'd pretend to be a risk analyst for a multi-national insurance company, a man who could predict one's likelihood for divorce. The people I met chuckled at the thought of this, but they all played along. They told me the number of sexual partners they'd had, the length of their marriage, the age difference between them and their spouse, and if there was any great disparity in earning power. Then they'd sit there silently while I scribbled on a cocktail napkin, waiting for the moment I'd slide it over and spin it around into view. "Forty-seven percent," I'd say. "Probably within the next five years. I should give you the name of my interpreter. I think you'd like Ukraine, I really do."

This is no way to achieve greater self-acceptance and serenity, though. To be on the defensive is to commit a sort of violence against one's self. To achieve true peace of mind and be released from one's anxieties, it is necessary to speak for the benefit of one's questioner rather than one's self. You have to let go and allow people to think of you as they will. It doesn't matter if to do this you must tell a lie; in the end, it's what everyone wants. Not to learn the truth but to believe they've been right all along.

I realized this the day I was browbeat by that woman at Dulles. "How old is she?" she asked. "*Fourteen?*" And so when she came back in her sensible shoes and those ridiculous Gaucho pants, I rose from my stool and handed her the bag of Duty Free she'd left behind, and I told her about Moldova and that lovely specimen I was returning to, the girl who hadn't understood at first why I'd put the money beneath her pillow, and then had thought it a queer thing to believe in, a tooth fairy. "She's fourteen," I said. "Would you believe it? Fourteen and the prettiest, most supple thing you'll ever see."

SOMETHING RED, SOMETHING BLUE

Tomlinson was in the jewelry store, following his fiancée from the expensive engagement rings to those costing twice as much, when he realized the full extent of his communist sympathies. This seemed an important thing to share with Monica, considering their many plans together and her job with the Chamber of Commerce. But she was already bent at the waist and pointing into the display case.

"There." She tapped the glass with the white tip of a manicured nail. "That's the one."

The saleswoman rose from one knee and offered the ring at the end of a delicately tilted wrist. "One of my favorites," she said, giving Tomlinson the smile of a dolphin.

Monica slipped the ring on and held her hand out at arm's length to admire the play of light on the stone. "It's not *gaudy* big, is it?"

She asked this while glancing back over one shoulder and smiling at her fiancé, but Tomlinson couldn't answer. He was too dazzled by the vibrancy of her teeth. She'd just had them done. Not bleached, done. Monica, he was beginning to realize, had everything done. Her nails, bi-monthly. Her teeth, bi-annually. And her breasts not even a month ago, in part because she otherwise didn't fit the wedding dress she'd liked most.

"Well? What do you think?"

Tomlinson lifted his eyes from her chest, and that was when he said it. "I'm a communist." Just like that. Like a streaker breaking onto the field.

Monica pulled her chin back and bunched her lips together in a squiggly line. She had imagined many things, Tomlinson knew. The invitations being misprinted, the caterer canceling the week of. One night the previous week she'd even said, "What if the minister's defrocked after declaring himself to be gay?" But never, not once, had she considered her fiancé announcing an affiliation with Vladimir Ilyich and the Red Chinese.

"You can't be serious," she said. "You're a realtor."

"Oh, no" – because it was real now, the words already spoken, the truth of them gaining shadow and depth – "I never wanted it. In college," he said, turning to the saleswoman, who reacted with a start, "I wanted to be an artist. Or maybe not an artist, but at least someone who doesn't wear a tie every day. Thought it might be nice to make chairs? You know, out of wood?" Tomlinson's cheek jumped. "Only my father" – and there he was again, dead of a heart attack at the age of fifty-five – "he said, 'Real Estate. Markets come and go, but people always need real estate.'"

"A communist?" Monica said. She pulled at the ring, yanking it off over the folds of her knuckle. "I'm sorry." She placed it in the cup of the saleswoman's hand and smiled apologetically. "It's his blood sugar. He always gets like this. I'm sure we'll be back after lunch."

She drove them to Restaurant Row, though Tomlinson insisted he wasn't hungry. "I had a late breakfast," he said. "Bliny."

"Crepes," Monica answered. "Don't give me bliny. You had crepes, or Swedish pancakes. Anything but bliny."

Tomlinson shrugged and looked out his window to all the mini-malls blurring by in the dreary August heat. Only he had left St.

Petersburg earlier that summer with a taste for bliny. Monica had hated everything about Russia, from the mobster who'd overcharged them for the taxi ride in from the airport to the mother she'd seen drinking beer while pushing her baby stroller down the sidewalk. She couldn't even drink the water – a sign at their hotel's check-in counter had informed them that St. Petersburg's pipes were teeming with *giardia*. "Don't look at me like I'm the Ugly American," she'd said that first night before bed, clutching her toothbrush in one hand. "I paid good money to come here, and where am I?" She sloshed sparkling water around inside her mouth, then spit a foamy white streak into the sink. "Back at French camp."

The thing was, Tomlinson enjoyed it. He loved waking knowing there'd be no hot shower, loved brushing his teeth with salty mineral water that tasted of the earth, and most of all he loved staying in at lunch with a plate of cheese and crackers and the sound of Shostakovich on the radio. It brought to mind the Great Patriotic War, when St. Petersburg had still been known as Leningrad and almost a million people had died during a nearly three-year-long Nazi blockade. The closest Tomlinson had come to such suffering and deprivation was the California energy crisis, when under the threat of rolling blackouts he'd been sure to turn his computer off at night.

"There's something wrong with that, don'tcha think? A sort of, I don't know, sense of entitlement?"

He said this as they stood beneath the painted frescoes of Kazan Cathedral. But Monica wasn't listening. She was digging through her purse, a large black satchel she'd twisted round and set before her like a pregnant woman's belly.

"I'm sorry, what?" She glanced up. "I can't find my camera. Didn't you give me the camera?"

Tomlinson shrugged, and changed the subject, and only expressed his anger outside, where a handful of withered old women were begging for change with silent looks of shame and defeat. Tomlinson stopped before one who was down on her knees and pressing her forehead into the sidewalk. She had supplicated herself before a gold-flecked icon painted onto chipped wood. "Oh you can't be serious," Monica said, after Tomlinson laid a 500 Ruble bill beside her. "They're everywhere," she said. "We could be doing this all day."

Tomlinson followed her without a word. They walked silently until they reached the Hermitage. But his mind was anything but quiet. For three years they'd been fine. For three years everything had been perfect, no second thoughts, but now he knew it – she wasn't the one. He knew it over his porridge the next morning at breakfast, just as he knew it with his bliny that day at lunch. She wasn't the one. It hurt to think this, because Tomlinson had thought the opposite for so long. But when the truth arrives, you can only submit to it. Three years he'd lost to this woman. Three years and she wasn't the one.

His breaking point came at the end of the week, when Monica, after announcing she'd be spending the morning in bed, asked him to bring her back a meatball sandwich from the Subway on Nevsky Prospekt. A fast food restaurant in Russia! Did she also want a KFC alongside the Mayan ruins, or a McDonald's Playland inside the Pyramid at Giza?

He left her with a kiss on the cheek, and took the stairs down to the lobby scowling like a third-rate Raskolnikov. Out on the sidewalk, he sidestepped pensioners with breastfuls of medals and plowed into tourists puzzling over their maps. At a bridge, he stopped to contemplate the drop velocity of a kopek, then moved off daydreaming of a train to Kiev or Minsk, where he saw for himself a new life with some thick-fingered Ludmilla, a woman who'd know what to do with a beet.

Near lunch, he followed a short flight of stone steps down into a little trinket shop beneath the sidewalk and stopped before a glass display case filled with Soviet-era medals. There were red stars and faces of Lenin, then flags of the USSR whipping in the wind. Tomlinson leaned in over the knick-knacks, thinking it all so very,

very sad. They hadn't seen it coming, not until it was too late; then the system collapsed, and what had replaced it? Ten years of poverty, crime and chaos. Monica thought capitalism had saved them; he believed it Russia's greatest mistake.

Tomlinson looked up as a woman approached holding something between the pinch of her fingers. A ring, he saw, as she set it down on the glass display case. He reached for it, gulping air like a diver coming up from the deep. It was a simple band, made of pliant metal – tin, he thought, as he held it up to his face – but it was beautiful in its simplicity, with two engraved roses, one circling this way, the other going that.

Tomlinson set the ring down and looked to the woman. She smiled, revealing a gold tooth. No English. For a sales pitch, this was it. He dropped his eyes back over the display case, looking past the ring now to a medal of Lenin beneath it. The revolutionary leader was shown in profile, his chin lifted, like a man looking into the future. Three years, Tomlinson thought, three years he'd been with her and who could say what would come next?

He reached for his wallet, wondering if ten dollars would do it, and then, not even two hours later, he was down on one knee, as sure of this as he had ever been sure of anything. "I love you," he said. "Will you be mine?"

The day after they visited the jewelry store, Tomlinson showed a house near the university to a couple that had three Ph.D's and not a decisive thought between them. He was thinking of getting a beer after, but on the drive back to the office he spotted a man protesting on a street corner. "Honk," his sandwich board read, "if you think dissent is patriotic!"

Tomlinson pulled up alongside him and pushed a button to lower his passenger-side window. The man took a few steps back, so

Tomlinson called out with a friendly partisan remark and waved him over. The man poked his head inside, nodding as he looked from the polished mahogany of the dashboard to the leather bucket seats that were stained the color of Tomlinson's latte, now cold and forgotten in the little holder by the stereo.

"These seats heat up?" he said. He smiled when Tomlinson nodded. "First time I sat in one of these, I thought I was peeing myself."

Tomlinson undid the top button of his oxford, saying it was a company car really, and that it kept the clients happy. "But listen, I wanted to ask if you knew if there was a chapter of the Communist Party in town."

"The Communist Party?"

Tomlinson said he'd checked the Yellow Pages and the web, but hadn't learned a thing. The man pulled his head out of the car and looked down the road as if ready to point toward a recognizable landmark. But then he shrugged and poked his head back inside, saying maybe it was illegal.

"Communism? No," Tomlinson said. "I think it's just frowned upon."

"What about the colleges then? Have you tried State?"

"There's nothing in the directory."

"And the university?"

"All the left-leaning kids are wearing green."

The man scratched himself inside his sandwich board. "I do know of a store," he said. "It might be worth a try."

Tomlinson reached for a pen and took the address down. Then after sharing a few dismal thoughts about the War on Terror, he was pulling back into traffic and driving toward The Cat and the Mouse.

The store did a brisk business in incense and sexual toys and water-based lube. He'd been there once before, in fact, when in an effort to enliven his and Monica's sex life, he'd asked for a pair of edible crotchless panties, only to discover that while they sold both edible and crotchless panties, they didn't sell any that were both edible and crotchless. "Why not just buy the edible," the clerk had suggested, "and eat the crotch out yourself?"

This afternoon, Tomlinson tossed his blazer onto the passenger seat and reached into the back of his BMW for a Che Guevara shirt he'd peeled off after a game of pick-up basketball the previous week. He got out of the car, then, ran a hand through his hair to give it that just-fucked/planning-a-revolution look, and made his way across the street.

Inside the store, he found a bulletin board over the rack of free newspapers. Bands were looking for drummers and bassists, feng shui consultants were eager to rearrange the contents of your room, and one massage therapist promised a vague but fulfilling time. There was nothing about the workers of the world uniting. The closest he could come was a pot-luck protest against the country's latest foreign policy outrage. But even that wouldn't do. Looking more closely, Tomlinson saw it had been held the previous fall.

He looked around, drawn next to the posters that were hanging from a display rack in back. He flipped through them and saw marijuana leaves and Led Zeppelin covers, posters of boy bands and pop princesses and one of a cat trying desperately to hang onto the branch of a tree. Then there they were, as unexpected and powerful as a revelation: Soviet-era propaganda posters. One showed a man holding out his hand to deny a shot of vodka. Nyet! Another had a downed American pilot, sharp-toothed and rabbit-faced, being led away from the smoldering wreckage of his plane by a barrel-chested Soviet soldier.

As he flipped through them, Tomlinson pictured the prints framed and hanging on the walls of a former barber shop located on Broadway. The shop had closed recently due to retirement or death, and was now listed in the MLS. He'd never thought to direct a client there (the price was right, the neighborhood wrong) but now he considered it for himself. It'd be the perfect location for a chapter of the Communist Party. It could be a community center of sorts, with the coffee always on and free literature available just inside the front door. He could even sell a few things to cover the cost of getting the message out. Shops selling records and coffee had already appeared up and down the street, and so if the young and disaffected were coming to Broadway for a Minor Threat album and a double half-caff cappuccino, why wouldn't they also stop by his place for a red skateboard and a CCCP T-shirt? Were there Marxist temporary tattoos? Didn't The Cat and the Mouse sell Soviet-themed novelty underwear? If he had to sell something, he'd rather it be this than McMansions and mini-malls. This could be the rest of his life, he realized. This could be the one thing he'd always wanted and never known.

But these thoughts were also interrupted. *Never again … I'm such an idiot … Fucking asshole.* A young woman spoke these words from behind the beaded curtain at his side, then pushed through, pocketing her cell-phone. Tomlinson dropped to one knee as she passed, and studied the shrink-wrapped poster tubes in the cubby holes beneath the display rack. She was a punk, maybe twenty-one or twenty-two, the type of person he could imagine frequenting his store: Germs T-shirt, pegged Levi's, tattoos and piercings, a generalized dissatisfaction with life.

He glanced over his shoulder. She was behind the front counter now, ringing up a customer. And she was beautiful, beautiful in her own way, with a face so pale Tomlinson suspected the use of a Japanese bleaching agent.

He fell in line behind two girls snickering over their purchase of Black Love incense. Then they were gone and the clerk was reaching for his poster, giving him just enough time to count her piercings – three in the nose, one in her cheek, another through her lip – before she could punch a few buttons on the register and say, "Seventeen fifty-three."

Tomlinson reached for his wallet and gave her a plastic card.

"Credit or debit?"

"Credit," he said, wanting to add something else, but it had been three years since he'd done this, three years since he'd first asked Monica out. "What do you think of the name 'Gorky Park?'" he said.

The girl tore the credit card receipt from the machine. "For what, a band?"

She thought it possible that he at thirty-three could be in a band! Was it the Che T-shirt? "No," he said. "A store, actually. You know, that sells communism stuff."

"You're opening a store that sells communism stuff?"

He shrugged. "There'd be some free literature as well, but yeah, to draw people in I thought I could sell skateboards and Soviet-era posters and what have you."

She pursed her lips and nodded. "How 'bout Red Square? Or's that too upscale?"

Tomlinson signed the receipt and slid the store copy back. They were both smiling now. "Might have to have to sleep on it. Come back and tell you what I think."

She told him to do that, and so Tomlinson left with a jaunty little wave of his poster, feeling so young and invigorated and reborn that on the drive home he hummed a vague approximation of the Soviet Union's national anthem. He'd watched the Olympics as a kid, and then there was that submarine movie starring Sean Connery, so he knew enough to give it a start. But after getting through the first few bars and swinging his arm to the beat of it, he merged onto the freeway and lost the tune completely. By the time he was pulling into the fast lane, he was belting out the Notre Dame fight song.

When Monica got home from work that night, Tomlinson was watching a documentary about Ivan the Terrible on the History Channel. He heard her behind him – putting something into the microwave, going through the mail, then approaching him to thrust a catalogue over his shoulder.

"Are you sure you'd prefer silver to gold?" she said.

He looked to the open page of the catalogue: engagement rings and wedding bands. He shrugged. Because what he really would have preferred was for her to be happy with the ring he'd bought in St. Petersburg. Not because he was cheap and didn't have the money, but because he wanted her to love him as if he were cheap and didn't have the money.

"Because I really do prefer gold," she said.

Tomlinson nodded, his eyes swinging back toward the television as a scream came from it. Ivan the Terrible's son fell to the floor, clutching his bloodied head. His father stood over him, holding a pointed staff, his face a stiffened mask of regret and over-acting. What did it matter anyway? Gold, silver, silver, gold. When had Monica ever listened to him? The sofa he sat on was plush white leather, though he preferred something firm, while the coffee table was a cold construction of chrome and glass rather a warm thing crafted out of wood. The microwave beeped, turning Monica back to the kitchen. Tomlinson looked to the O'Keefe on the wall. Vaginal. There was no other word for it. He was like a man living in the waiting room of a gynecologist's office.

"You want me to use the ring you bought me," Monica said. "That's what this is all about. Right?"

He heard her pull out a chair at the table and sit down.

"It's made of tin," Monica said. "You do know that? I mean, it's a nice gesture and all, very romantic, but you do know it's made of tin?"

Tomlinson turned on the sofa and spoke over one shoulder, telling her what he had learned through two other shoppers in the store, after the story had been translated from Russian to French to English. "That ring saved someone's life. It was made by a prisoner in the gulags, just after the war. That ring was given to a guard in exchange for another slice of bread, or another scoop of soup. It's very possible that ring saved someone's life."

Monica's dinner steamed before her; she sat with her arms crossed. "It's fucking tin," she said.

That evening in bed, Tomlinson read Lenin's *What's to Be Done?* while Monica flipped through that month's *Cosmo*.

"Did you know there was no graffiti in communist countries?" he said. "And that crime rates were so low there wasn't a street a woman didn't dare walk down alone?"

"I know you're not stupid enough to try to convert me," Monica said, "so let me just remind you that if you spray-painted 'Clapton is God' on a statue of Lenin they locked you up for fifty years and gave your wife electro-shock."

Tomlinson dropped his book off the side of the bed; Monica set her magazine on the bedside table and reached for the light. Then Tomlinson lay there, thinking of the girl he'd met that day and seeing her bleached-white face alongside his as they hung posters in the barber shop on Broadway. He fantasized about sex on the floor and a position he'd never tried. It was enough to give him the start of an erection, and so he rolled over toward Monica, thinking to reach for her breasts. Sex. That's what could pull them out of this. Vigorous, healthy, angry sex. But his mind wouldn't cooperate. At the thought of Monica's new breasts, those plastic, payment-plan breasts, Tomlinson pictured his fiancée in a concentration camp, a gulag, on the day of its liberation. Like the other prisoners, she was emaciated after a long stay, but while her face was gaunt and her stomach had pulled in beneath her exposed ribs, her breasts had remained the same. High, firm, round. The tits of a teenager.

Tomlinson rolled back in the other direction, telling himself it was just as well. It had been – he counted this in his head – twenty-three days since she'd had the procedure, and still he hadn't seen the results. She wouldn't let him. They were too sensitive, she'd said. It even hurt to expose her breasts to the light and the air, so she'd kept them hidden away from him all this time, like Heather and Julie, her two most neurotic friends.

Things progressed like this, sexless and strained, for more than a week. Tomlinson spent his days showing houses that had million dollar asking prices; then nights, usually after a trip to The Cat and The Mouse, he came home to a bowl of rice and beans and ignored Monica's offers for wine. Monica matched Tomlinson's silent aggression with a mute denial of her own. She saw the poster tubes accumulating in the back of their walk-in closet, but she ignored them until they were lined up like rifles at an armory.

"Okay, I give. What is it?" She stepped out of the closet one morning holding a tube up like a sword. "You want to redecorate? Is that it?"

Tomlinson sat on the foot of the bed with his hands on his knees. He was dressed for work (loafers, khakis, an oxford and a red tie), but that only meant so much. After knotting his tie the previous day, all he'd done was hang out at the 7-Eleven and try to convince a Pakistani immigrant and a stoned high-school drop-out to stop selling donuts and demand a living wage.

Tomlinson looked up. The top three buttons of Monica's silk blouse were undone, partially exposing the lace of her white brassiere. He lifted his chin as if to peer over a brick wall. She pulled the poster out from its tube and saw enough to catch its political intent, then pushed it back down and tossed it aside.

"I come home each night thinking you've left me," she said. "Do you know that? I've started telling people that when we get married, you'll be my something blue. But I don't know anymore. I'm starting to wonder if even that is too optimistic."

Tomlinson looked away, shaking his head. What could he say? He didn't even know what was wrong. "I spoke to a friend from college the other day," he told her. "He said a communist revolution couldn't ever work here. He said in a country with delivery pizza and twenty-four hour porn, the political spectrum is inherently narrowed."

Monica sat down beside him and patted his thigh. "We'll get through this," she said. "Every couple goes through this."

"I'm a communist," he said. "You're a Republican. We've never debated water-boarding."

"I know."

He looked her in the eyes. "I want to talk to you about torture."

"There's time for that."

"And Guantanamo Bay."

"We'll talk about that and the gulag too. Just tell me that you love me. Do you love me?"

Tomlinson nodded. Tomlinson smiled. But then he also started to cry.

Monica stood and walked to the dresser, where she grabbed her purse and started looking around for her keys. When she'd found them, her eyes were wet too. "What kind of answer," she said, turning to him at the door while pulling a Kleenex from her purse. "What kind of answer is that?" And then she pressed the Kleenex into the corner of one eye and left saying he had until the end of the day.

"For what?" Tomlinson asked, too soft for her to hear, and then the door was closing between them.

Tomlinson went into the kitchen and fixed a bowl of Women's Health cereal, the only box left on the shelf; then he took his breakfast into the living room and turned on the TV. The sofa ruined it. He sank into the white leather until his knees rose up before his eyes. On the coffee table were two copies of *Oprah* magazine and a book no bigger than his hand that offered ancient Toltec wisdom and a practical guide to personal freedom. He glanced at the O'Keefe on the wall – vaginal, still – then set his bowl down.

The doorbell rang. UPS. He signed his name and walked back into the living room tearing at the box. A Marx T-shirt inside, one he'd bought online from the Communist Party USA's website and had delivered express. He took off his oxford while a morning news program played on TV, then kicked off his penny loafers and stepped out of his khakis and pulled off his brown socks, too. For a moment, he stood there in only his boxers. Then he put on his new T-shirt and went into his room for his favorite Levi's and the pair of Doc Martens he'd worn in college.

When he got to The Cat and the Mouse, Opal (he had learned the clerk's name was Opal) was sucking on a lollipop and inspecting the contents of the front display case alongside a co-worker. Tomlinson passed with a nod hello, grabbed the one remaining poster he hadn't yet purchased from the back, then circled round toward the register.

The second clerk was sitting on his haunches and making notes on a clipboard as he peered in at the shelves.

"We out of the Kobe Tai?" he said.

Opal shook her head. "The Jenna Jameson." She pulled her lollipop out of her mouth so she could speak more clearly. "Doggy-style."

Tomlinson looked more closely at the display case. The top two shelves held "portable pussies" and "vibrating vaginas," all constructed from plastics and synthetics and promising to be modeled upon the exact genital likeness of this porn star or that. Opal smiled when she caught him looking.

"*Perestroika,*" she said, in a bad Russian accent. "*Da?*"

Tomlinson looked up confused.

"For the name of your shop," she said. "*Perestroika.*"

"Oh. Yeah." He nodded briskly to keep from having to say anything else, and laid his credit card down to complete a purchase he no longer wanted to make. It was a question of timing more than anything. If they'd restocked the sex toys five minutes earlier, it would have been fine. If they'd done it five minutes after he left, all would have been well and good. But now? It left him feeling like the saddest man in a brothel, the one who realizes his mistake too late – that he has come here of all places looking for love.

"Credit or debit?"

"Debit," he said.

Tomlinson returned to his condo a little before six and followed the smell of cooked meat into the kitchen. Monica was already home. He met her in the bedroom, as she emerged from the shower wet and glistening and wrapped in a plush white towel.

"You're cooking?" he said. She cooked like the pilgrims once bathed: maybe twice a year.

"Just a roast." Monica toweled her hair dry, nodding but not meeting his eye. "I thought we should try. You know, after all this time."

He felt so ashamed. He was the one who should be apologizing, and yet she was the one home early and preparing a feast. He pulled off his t-shirt while walking into the closet. "I don't know where to start," he said. "This morning" – he kicked out of his shoes – "I've just been so ... God."

He turned round toward her, dressed now in only his blue jeans, and stopped after a single step back into the bedroom. Monica was half-nude. She stood over her bath towel in the center of the floor, lit up by the last of the sun coming in through the blinds. Her breasts were on full display, showing no signs of bruising or the knife. And they were magnificent. Tomlinson had to admit it, even though he hadn't been the one to propose the procedure – had in fact argued against it. But no, now he saw the end result, and it was magnificent. Magnificent and huge.

"Something borrowed," she said, "something red."

And hearing this, Tomlinson's eyes dropped to her panties, which were red, revolutionary red and decorated by a gold hammer and sickle.

He walked toward her unbuttoning his jeans, because it had been weeks now, months almost – far, far too long – but now here it was at last. He got down on his knees before her. He held her hips in his hands, first kissing the point of one hip-bone and then the other. Monica placed her hands in his hair. She closed her eyes to focus on the pleasure. And then Tomlinson pulled at her panties, and he brought them down, down like a revolution.

VLADIMIR'S MUSTACHE

They were lined up outside the door to the Actor's Union, seated in chairs on either side of the hall. There was Dima and Tolya, Ilya and Luka, and that bore Vladimir Antonovich Pugachov, who would never cease to remind you that he had studied at the feet of Stanislavski himself. Boris Nikolayevich lifted his hat to say hello, but he received only a few nods of recognition in return. Everyone was going over their lines. The hallway buzzed with that earnest mumbling peculiar to Jews in prayer and actors before an audition.

Boris walked to the office at the end of the hall and grabbed the clipboard that hung from a string. He added his name to the list, then turned, looking for an empty chair – halfway back in the direction he'd started. As he moved toward it, he realized that all the actors had dark hair. A decade earlier, he would have noticed this when he reached the top of the landing. But a decade earlier he would not have been out of breath after only three flights of stairs, and so his skills of observation were the least to change.

Boris fell into a seat with a groan and took off his hat to wipe his brow with a handkerchief. At his left sat an actor who'd returned from a camp in the North. While the others had dug a canal, he had put on plays for the guards and the inmates. He had been beaten when he forgot his lines, but then it was not whether or not you were beaten, he'd said, only why. With such words, Boris was sure the man would be going back, if not to a camp in the North, then one to the east. He looked at the man across from him: Vladimir Antonovich, his co-worker at the Moscow Air Field and the man with whom he shared a communal apartment on the outer edge of the new Metro line. Vladimir Antonovich had worn a full beard at breakfast, but since then he'd shaved all but a tiny patch of hair – a mustache no larger than the shadow beneath his nose. Boris wanted to laugh. He wanted to throw his elbow into the ribs of the man next to him and point. "Look at my neighbor," he wanted say. "Do you see!" But he also wished his eyes had not opened on such a thing, for with the threat of Fascist Germany growing in the West, Boris could only think it must be a crime to wear Vladimir's mustache this side of Minsk.

He threw his handkerchief into the crown of his hat and slid his feet out before him. He had not even stopped by the previous week to pick up a copy of the script. But then why bother? It was just another propaganda film, and for five years now the formula had been the same: Overcome this hardship, survive that, remember always the glory of the state. It was maddening. He wanted a part. Something he could sink his teeth into. Something worthy of his three years of study at the State Red Flag Theater for Russian Drama. But no, he got cast as a peasant, always a peasant. Take this sickle, they said, go into that field. Now sing a patriotic song and stand proud like the New Soviet Man. He swatted the air – "Bah!" – and only realized he'd said this aloud when Vladimir Antonovich glanced up from his script and squinted, causing his mustache to arch like a caterpillar.

Boris's smile bounced. "My wife," he said, "she asks that I go to the market, but this is women's work, I tell her." Again, he swatted the air – "Bah!" – and with this Vladimir Antonovich nodded and returned to his lines.

Boris pulled his hat down over his eyes. Sleep, that is what he needed. To disappear from this place and sleep.

When he awoke it was to a voice calling his name: "Boris Nikolayevich Ivanov!"

He sat up blinking and pushed back on his hat. Vladimir Antonovich came hurtling down the hall toward him, his hand clamped tightly over his mustache as if he were gathering the courage to pull it off.

"Boris Nikolayevich Ivanov!"

Boris stood, bumping shoulders with Vladimir Antonovich as he passed, and strode off after the woman who'd called his name. She dropped the clipboard on its string and turned into the Union Hall. When he met her inside, Boris was handed a script and pointed to a podium at the front of the room.

"A podium?" he said.

"For your speech," she said.

He nodded slowly, the adrenaline of his mad dash now gone. He should have expected this: Art reduced to messages, acting turned into a simple recitation of the lines. These were the times, after all, and so as he walked behind the podium, he wondered what they would have him do if he got the part. Tour the farms by train? Give lectures from Moscow to Kiev, praising collectivization and damning the *kulak*? Well, he would do it. He would do it if they asked because at least it meant he wouldn't have to push a broom, that he could stay at home and learn his lines and leave the rest to Vladimir Antonovich and Old Man Petrushkin at the Air Field.

"Will I be reading alone?" he asked.

The woman nodded, seated now behind a table that was shared by a man with a blue nose and a red scarf. The director. Boris didn't recognize him. But then what did it matter who directed what when not one line of dialogue could be changed without two rubber stamps? It had happened on a film he had been cast in back in '35 or '36. The director had insisted on changing some dialogue, and so the rewritten lines (there were only three) had been sent to the Central Administration of Literature and Publishing, where they remained for fifteen months. When the script came back, with its binding sealed in red wax and CALP stamped across its front, the director and the actors had gathered round a table to read through the now largely forgotten work, and it was then that the director realized he preferred the lines the way they had originally been written. "I see that now," he said. "It was much better, was it not?" And it was, they all agreed. But the lines were also no longer approved, no matter if they had been only fifteen months previous. So the script was returned to the Central Administration, where it promptly disappeared, as did the director.

Boris looked for the name of the writer on the title page, then squeezed his eyes closed, reminding himself that this too was meaningless. After all, a country of artists had entered the First All-Union Congress of Soviet Writers – Kirshon, Nikolai Pogodin, the great playwright Nikitin – but only one had emerged: the New Soviet Man. And so now while the setting of a movie might change from a factory to a farm, or even blast off into outer space, the story line never changed. There was the politically conscious worker and the one who believed not in the values of the state. From there the formula was simple: unmask, catch, and execute the *kulak* or saboteur. Do this with the wise counsel of a member of the Communist Party and the approval of an older worker who supplies the same tired Bolshevik jokes. It was enough to make Boris wish for the courage to escape to Hollywood, where at least movies – or no, films – were made for the pure true sake of art.

He cleared his throat. "From the top?"

The director nodded.

Boris turned the page and read:

FADE IN:

INT. AUDITORIUM - BERLIN - DAY

Where NAZI FLAGS and SWASTIKAS decorate a stage filled by NAZI LEADERS and GESTAPO OFFICERS.

HITLER appears on-stage to the CHEERS of an ADORING CROWD. He approaches a PODIUM, and waits for the silence that will allow his speech to begin.

Boris Nikolayevich looked up, his eyes as soft and misty as they had been the day he'd dropped to one knee before his wife. Hitler? He could play Hitler? Because this was a part, this was a part worthy of three years of study at the State Red Flag Theater for Russian Drama!

The director twirled a hand over his head. "When you are ready."

"Yes," Boris told him, "yes," and here he counted to three and breathed deeply through his nose, regaining his composure as he straightened his back and lifted his chin. His face hardened. He used the palm of one hand to pat down the front forelock of his hair. Then it began. And when he launched into the lines, his voice was so powerful, so full of spittle and hate, it could have brought hail from above and risen the dead from below. He gestured, he slapped at the podium and clawed at the air, denounced the Jew and the Communist, the Communist and the Jew, and broke off only once to say, "Wait, can I do that again? I would like to try something different when I say 'communist.'"

It was a command performance. His throat grew hoarse from the fury of it all. And when the director came out from behind his desk, looking so grim it could only mean he was happy, Boris Nikolayevich Ivanov knew he had the part before they were even shaking hands.

Boris had not studied at the Moscow Art Theater like his co-worker Vladimir Antonovich, but he had read of the methods developed by its director, the great Stanislavski. The Muscovite had brought a revolution to the stage just as Lenin had brought a revolution to the fields. No longer would an actor trod out before the audience to deliver his lines with all the wooden honesty of a prince or a politician. The Slow Feet of Sorrow. The Radiant Mask of Joy. The Clenched Fists of Fury. These were now obsolete, replaced by the depths of psychology – a complicated inner-life that made a character not just understood but believed.

As Boris rode the tram to Sverdlov Square, he searched his memory for those experiences in his life that could help launch him into the physical body of the feared German leader. He had a younger brother, Misha, one whom in his youth he had ordered around, telling him to fetch his shoes and be quiet and run to the kiosk for mother. But was this enough? Where else could he look?

Boris stepped off the tram at Petrovka Street, getting out beneath a red banner that hung from a lamp-post and bore an image of Stalin's face. He approached the many flower vendors gathered around Sverdlov Square and inspected them as he imagined Hitler might: walking from one to the next with his hands behind his back, and stopping occasionally to admire a rose or offer a few paternal words. "Mother Russia needs more women like you," he told one vendor. "Tell me," he asked another, "do you not think the Russian people more equipped to admire beauty than those of the Germanic races? Is there not something in our souls more sensitive?"

Before yet another woman, he reached into a bucket for a rose that was neither white nor purple but a marbling of the two. He looked up from it to find the round face of the woman selling it. She smiled. But Boris Nikolayevich was not happy. "It is a mongrel," he said, before reaching for another – a red rose, a true classic beauty – that he brought up to his nose while praising its color and scent. "I will take three," he said, and as he turned to leave the woman reached for his elbow, reminding him in a tone Hitler never heard that he had better not forget to pay.

After entering his seventh-floor apartment, Boris filled a glass vase with water and arranged the flowers on the kitchen table. Beside them, he left the packet of lamb he'd bought at the market. His wife had requested pork, but with his good fortune that day, Boris had thought it excusable to go for the extravagance.

He checked his watch: Lena would be home soon, and no doubt Vladimir Atonovich and his wife as well. He took his script to the balcony, and there sank into a wooden chair and with a pencil went over his lines. His part was not the biggest. He appeared in only three scenes, and then as only a backdrop to the main story of a Communist family that was treated poorly (and ultimately killed) in a large unnamed German city. But even if he had fewer lines than Yuri, the oppressed worker who takes heroic and collective action, and Natasha, his strong but humble wife – and not even as many as Otto, the cruel factory foreman – he saw he had room for the type of nuance and interpretation that could allow his character to steal the show.

"Concentrate on your breathing here," he wrote in the margin of page two. "This should be bold, yes," he added on twelve, "but do not forget his vulnerability. Hitler is our enemy, but a human being too."

When he looked up from his read-through, the sun had fallen behind the apartment tower across from his own and a row of pigeons had gathered on his balcony's ledge. He stood and addressed these cooing birds with the lines of his second scene, which came on page thirteen and showed Hitler meeting with a group of industrialists in the winter of '33.

"For more than a decade," he said, "the German nation has been subjected to the injustices of Versailles. Our people have suffered. They have cashed their paychecks at lunch, fearing they would be worthless by supper – and this only if they had a job." Boris dropped his right fist into the palm of his left hand, scaring a bird from the balcony with his rising voice. "In such a world," he said, "it is understandable that so many would turn to the message of the Communist. Understandable," he said, as the remaining birds lifted with flight, "but not tolerable. We cannot tolerate Communism, gentlemen. We must drive the Communist out!"

In the script, the scene ended with the applause of the industrialists, but here it was instead interrupted by the sound of shattering glass – his wife stood at the door, the three flowers he'd bought her now lying at her feet among the remains of the vase.

"What are you doing?"

Boris reached to the seat behind him for his script (he was quick to get off book, a talent he usually found no reason to regret) and waved the manuscript up by the side of his face. "Rehearsing." He tried a smile. "I got the part."

Lena crouched down to pick up the flowers and turned inside, saying what did she care of this part, if this was how he talked.

Boris stepped over the broken glass and followed her in, catching up to his wife as she laid the flowers on the table and grabbed the packet of meat he'd left for her. He circled his arms around her waist and kissed her neck, saying she should be happy. "Now I can stay at home and rehearse."

But she just as quickly broke free from his hold – slapping at the script he held rolled in his hands – and crossed to the kitchen counter unwrapping the meat. "And now you'll be doing more of the same? What was that out there? I heard you say things the Pugachovs could have heard if they were home, even the Petrushkins down the hall." She slammed the meat down onto a wooden cutting board and reached for a heavy knife.

Boris stood at her back, his hand half-raised in the air. "That was very expensive," he said. "Lamb chops, not pork."

Lena slammed the blade down between two bones. "Obviously," she said, turning to point the tip of her knife, "you are not a peasant. Or maybe this shouting I heard is not from the lines in your script but the thoughts in your head – at least tell me it's not that! Do you even remember we live in a *kommunalka*? That we share this apartment with others who are neither deaf nor dumb? What would they think? What's gotten into you, Borya?"

He stood before her, smiling as if being told to hold the pose for the camera. "I am Hitler," he said.

And Lena looked at him as she had the day he'd dropped to one knee, with a looseness in her jaw and a softness in her eyes. "Hitler?" she said.

Boris glanced back to the flowers on the table. Usually he bought his wife only one, but today he'd been so happy he'd bought three. Still, it wasn't enough, he knew, not with their communal apartment. Lena wished that they would join the Party. They could have a better life, she'd said, maybe even a flat in the city center. But you had to be asked to join, and Boris had spent his youth not with the revolution but on the stage. Maybe if he were named a People's Artist of the Soviet Union – maybe then he could satisfy his wife. But planning for this was like planning for the answer to a prayer. No artist was so named without Stalin's blessing.

"I will be a very good Hitler," he said, thinking this might somehow please her. But then Lena turned back to the meat with another whack of her knife.

"And why lamb? Are we Jews now? Muslims? Why no pork? Do we live in Tashkent?"

Boris turned away from her as she continued her assault. "The best Hitler I can be," he said, though now these words were mumbled to himself, mumbled and lost to the wind as he returned to the balcony and silently looked about for the birds.

It was not the celebration he had imagined. After dining on the lamb chops (which Boris thought Lena purposely burnt) they went to the cinema, if only to sit together in the dark. Boris dozed through the opening, seeing enough to know the film was set in a factory, not on a farm, and that it involved a saboteur this time, not a *kulak*. But then he jerked awake in his seat and laughed nervously as the audience gasped: it was not a fellow factory worker who unmasked the saboteur, but the man's very own wife – a woman who had already pledged to him her undying love.

Boris looked to Lena as if to share with her the smile that follows an awkward joke. But his wife refused to acknowledge him. Her eyes were fixed on the screen, where the saboteur's wife was crying in the office of the local Communist Party chief. This man leaned across his desk and gave the woman his handkerchief, and when the woman saw what she held, her tears stopped and her eyes turned to take in the small flag on his desk, which like the handkerchief was red.

"I understand now," she said, her eyes moving to a painting of Stalin that hung from a wall. "With class struggle, Communism will spread across the globe." She wiped her tears and stood. "I must give everything to the revolution."

The Commissar came out from behind his desk and took her hands in his. He looked down into her eyes, her bosom heaving. "I must praise," he said, "your fine proletariat spirit."

Boris leaned over to whisper in his wife's ear: "I will just use the men's room." He did not want to see the trial scene that surely followed, nor the execution that would come after that. "The lamb," he said, "I think it has touched me wrong. I will wait in the lobby."

And Lena nodded, keeping her eyes on the screen.

The next morning, Boris snuck into the Moscow Airport with all the caution of a common thief, doing this so he would not be detected by his co-workers. He entered the supply closet in Hangar #2 and pulled the string to engage the light. It was in this room, behind the many stacks of toilet tissue (brown for domestic flights, white for diplomatic) that Boris had hidden a copy of Shakespeare's *Hamlet*. Each day between departures and arrivals he stole a few minutes alone with it, acting on a stage that measured four foot by four foot and was surrounded on three sides by wooden shelves rather than tiers of box seats. The lighting was harsh (a single exposed bulb overhead) and his costume (blue coveralls tied at the waist with a string) required a modern interpretation of the Bard's work. But at least here he could make that interpretation, for the Prince of Denmark had not been brought to life elsewhere in the Soviet Union for several years, unless other closets were home to other such performances. "Hamlet is always being and not-being," Stalin is rumored to have said, "and what can the proletariat understand of this when always they simply are?"

This morning, Boris did not reach for *Hamlet*; he reached for Hitler instead. After breathing deeply to sink into his new body, he postured and posed, inflated his chest and turned this way and that, first with his hands on his hips, then with them flying through the air as if conducting a symphony of rage. "In such a world," he said, returning to the scene he had rehearsed on his balcony, "it is understandable that so many would turn to the message of the Communist. Understandable," he said, "but not tolerable. We cannot tolerate Communism, gentlemen – we must drive the Communist out! For how can we appeal to national unity when half the German people wish to raise the flag of the Bolshevik to the east? No act of legislation will help us, only an iron will. Without it, the Asiatic mob will overrun our German streets and there will go our culture and our business, our foundations of morality, and our very notion of Fatherland! We have suffered as a nation for more than a decade, but even this could not be compared to the misery of a Germany from which the red flag of destruction has been raised!"

"What are you doing?"

Boris turned, one hand still raised before him like a claw. It was Vladimir, Vladimir Antonovich interrupting his performance at the door.

"Why are you here? You got the part. You should be home rehearsing."

Boris stepped to one side as Vladimir pushed into the closet and then backed out with two brooms. He did not know what to say. He stood there. He lowered his hand.

"Here." Vladimir Antonovich gave him one of the brooms. "And grab some toilet paper. We don't have time for this. If you plan to stay, work. A plane is arriving from Berlin."

Boris followed his neighbor out, telling him that Lena had thought he was too loud to rehearse at home. "It would be a bother to you and your wife, we thought. But I will gladly work," he said. "I will certainly help you clean the planes, if only between flights I can perhaps have a few minutes alone. To rehearse my lines, I mean. Back in the closet. Do you think?"

Vladimir Antonovich grunted as they emerged from the hangar and moved out beneath the clouded skies. A silver plane turned in off the runway, guided to its parking strip by Old Man Petrushkin, who stood stooped and waving two bright orange handles. Vladimir Antonovich stopped next to a wheeled staircase used to disembark passengers. He planted his broom at his side with a soldier's discipline, while Boris fell in at his side and leaned into the handle of his own.

"I must tell you, Vladimir Antonovich. You are a very fine actor. I envy your talents."

"You do not need to tell me this," Vladimir Antonovich said, turning to speak over the roar of the approaching plane. "I studied at the feet of Stanislavski himself!"

Boris nodded, raising his voice against the sound of the propellers. "Perhaps it is just that you were too tall!"

"What?"

"For Hitler! Almost two meters! And who could believe a Hitler like that?!"

Vladimir Antonovich shook his head. "I am not jealous, if that is what you believe! It is only that I have fears!"

"What?"

"Fears! That it pleases you not to be cast in a part, but to be cast in this part!"

The plane's roar was deafening. Boris's hair blew atop his head. Oh? his expression said.

"My wife spoke with yours last night, and she is as certain as I."

"They spoke?" Boris said.

"How else to explain the ease with which you fall into the role? You enjoy playing Hitler," he said, and now the propellers were sputtering to a stop, "that much is clear, and tell me, what kind of Soviet enjoys that?"

Old Man Petrushkin had heard the last of this while shuffling over from the parking strip. "The type of Soviet," he joked, poking one of his orange handles into Boris's chest, "that won't be playing Hitler very long."

It was a tired joke, a variation of one he had told too many times before, but Vladimir Antonovich laughed as if it were the very invention of humor. Boris managed a brave smile. Then, as the propellers thumped to a stop, Boris's co-workers were off, pushing the wheeled staircase into the fuselage of the plane.

Moments later, as the sun moved between two clouds and began to play against the plane's hammered silver surface, the cabin door swung open from inside and Foreign Minister Molotov stepped out.

Only then did Boris sprint toward the plane with a soldier's precision, holding the broom out before him like a rifle and realizing his mistake. He had grabbed the wrong sheets of toilet paper – brown, not white – and so as the raised claw to Stalin's fist of steel moved down toward the tarmac, Boris fell in alongside his co-workers, pushing the sheets of paper deep down inside his back pocket.

That evening, after Vladimir Antonovich's wife served him a dinner of borsch, Boris tried to sleep and couldn't. He got up at one o'clock, and a little before three, and then again at four-thirty. He read on the balcony, tried to sedate himself with heavy food, and finally resorted to the bottle. The last of this – three long gulps of vodka – proved effective, though not even two hours later his wife was up with the sun and frying sausage and telling him he shouldn't be late.

Boris pushed up on his elbows and returned the word to her as a question: Late? He did not have to work until the movie was completed. He said he would maybe just ride the tram.

Lena appeared at the door to their room holding the frying pan. "Is there trouble at work? Yesterday you said you could rehearse at work."

"There is no more trouble there," Boris said, "than there is here. But it is difficult. You must understand."

"I understand that if you think you'll rehearse on the tram, you don't understand what people will think. You can't sit there murmuring like you do, not of Hitler and all the rest. They'll pull you from your seat and drag you to the *militsiya*."

"Then I will stay here," Boris said.

Before Lena could answer, there was another voice calling out to them from Lena's rear – it was Vladimir Antonovich's wife opening the far door and moving into the kitchen, saying she smelled sausage she couldn't see. "One minute!" Lena called to her, before stepping further inside her own room and telling her husband with a firm whisper that he had better not stay here.

"I can be quiet," Boris said. "I will stay in this room and whisper my lines."

"Hitler can be quiet?" Lena's voice was no louder than his, but somehow more forceful. "Hitler the German? The Hitler I know does not whisper!"

"Elena Alexandrovna!" It was Vladimir Antonovich. "I respectfully ask if I need chain my own wife to the stove to be fed this beautiful morning?"

Boris rolled over in bed. "Where can I go, then?" Filming was not set to begin for several weeks, but he had to prepare and formal rehearsal space was not available for another three weeks. He popped up on his elbows. "Tell me, where is it safe? Where can I go?"

Boris's wife looked at him. She didn't have an answer. She shook her head, as if dismissing him or dismissing this, he wasn't sure, and at last turned back for the kitchen. Boris heard her set the plates on the table and tell Vladimir Antonovich there was no coffee this morning, only tea. Then she called to him that his food was getting cold, and so he got up and joined them, sat and ate, the morning passing without conversation until the others had left. "Drink your tea," his wife said then. "Eat your sausage," she said. "The Ferris wheel."

Boris looked up from his plate at the last of these words.

"The Ferris wheel," she said. "You can rehearse while riding the Ferris wheel at the Park of Culture and Rest."

Boris rode the Metro to the Park Kultury station, then took the escalator up toward the street, not looking at the red posters framed and hanging on the walls.

At the entrance, he pushed through the glass doors and saw three members of the *militsiya* approaching. He looked behind him as if he'd been followed, then glanced back to the fore to see if he was wrong and was in fact being met. But no, this was only paranoia. They passed by him and pushed through the doors, soon off into the Metro's lower depths.

Boris walked into the sunshine and crossed the street. He was not certain how it would happen, if it would be his wife to denounce him or his neighbors, perhaps Vladimir Antonovich at work, but if not the one then the other, and sooner rather than later – of this much he was certain.

Boris entered the park and walked down a path picking up red mud on his boots. He muttered first about his suspicions (it would be his wife, because then she could marry again, maybe find herself a man in the Party) and then about his mutterings (instead of doubting his wife's pledge of love he should be honoring his own and rehearsing).

He tried to fall into character. He set his hands behind his black overcoat and stiffened his face, nodding to a young woman who passed at the controls of a baby's pram. But it was too late. Already he was reaching the gate in front of the Ferris wheel, where the old man who served as the ride's conductor sat serenely on a wooden stool. To the man's side was a sign advertising the price in peeling red on white paint: 20 kopeks. Boris glanced between it and the conductor, thinking the old man looked as he had once imagined God must look, like Tolstoy in old age, with a full white beard and skin so clear and pure it resembled nothing more than trapped light.

The old man rose from his stool and smiled. He was as patient as the day.

"I am in mourning," Boris thought to say. "My young wife, I proposed to her here, but now she is dead" – he reached into his wallet for a thick clump of bills and thrust them toward the conductor – "and I only want to ride the Ferris wheel all day to remember."

The old man placed two hands around Boris's one and said, "*Tovarish*, please, keep your money. We are like one heart beating together as one, for I too have lost my bride, my dear and lovely Vika, wife of fifty-three years. Please."

He swung the gate open, then walked with Boris to a waiting green carriage and closed the little door behind him. It was not the weekend. The park was not filled with lovers and children, just a few old women and men sitting on far-off benches. The only one to join Boris on the Ferris wheel was a pigeon which fluttered to a stop on the railing of the red carriage next to his own. Boris held his tongue until the old man had turned and walked away; then he whispered at the bird: "Go! Go away! Get!"

His words did not persuade the creature, but the conductor's hand did. When the old man pulled back on a lever, the Ferris wheel lurched and swung into a counter-clockwise orbit, and with this first burst of energy, the pigeon squawked and jumped and disappeared. Boris pulled his script out from his overcoat and sat with it in his lap. On the first go-round, he was content to admire the view of the city, the capital spread out in front of him beyond the Moscow River. The second time around, he whispered his lines from three o'clock to nine, when he was sure the old man could not hear him. Then on his third orbit, more comfortable still, he rose to his feet and returned to the scene he'd last abandoned at the airport.

"We have suffered as a nation for more than a decade. But even this could not be compared to the misery of a Germany from which the red flag of destruction has been raised." It sounded wrong; he knew it. He was sad today, not full of hate. He needed fury and fight, a sharpness to his voice, not rounded edges. Boris pounded his fist into the flat of one hand, throwing his body erect and stomping the floor with one foot. "For if a decade of Marxism has ruined Germany, one year of Bolshevism will surely destroy her!" The carriage swung from side to side as he stomped and he spat and his arms flew out around him. "Lend me your strength, gentlemen, for we must be unified if we are to throw out the Communist and march forward to raze Moscow, and it is this that we must do – we must raze the Russian capital to the ground and turn the city into a giant reservoir, a reservoir in which no memory of Marx or Lenin shall remain!"

He was possessed. He held his clenched fists up at his sides, had white spittle in the corners of his mouth, and wore the frozen look of a snarling death mask. Only then did he realize his mistake: he was standing at ground level, the ride having brought him full circle, the ride having brought him to a complete stop.

The carriage swung gently from left to right, still swayed by his momentum.

The old man stood, knocking over his short wooden stool. "You!" he said, his hand stretching out between them. "You!"

Boris shook his head. He did this and tried to speak. But he could not answer the accusation. He'd spent all his words.

The old man pulled at the ride's lever, sending the Ferris wheel spinning up away from this earth. Boris retook his seat and stared off into the distance, out over the Moscow River. The *militsiya* would soon appear, running up the same red path the old man now hobbled down, their batons swinging at their belts. But even when they came into view, even then Boris did not look. The part for him was already cast, but he was not ready for the call. So he sat like an actor awaiting an audition, his lips moving quietly as if in prayer, until at last the lever was pulled again, and the wheel came spinning to a halt.

ACKNOWLEDGMENTS

The following stories have been previously published, in some cases in a slightly different form: "Kamkov the Astronomer" in *The Cincinnati Review*; "The Castrato of St. Petersburg" in *Salt Hill*; "Vladimir's Mustache" in *Ninth Letter*; "The Lady with the Stray Dog" in *Witness*; "Yagoda's Bullets" in *Drunken Boat*; "Something Red, Something Blue" in *Low Rent*; and "The Secret Meeting of the Secret Police" in *Night Train*.

ABOUT THE AUTHOR

Stephan Eirik Clark's short stories have appeared in numerous literary magazines, including *Ninth Letter*, *Witness*, *The Cincinnati Review*, and *LA Weekly*, and been nominated for a Pushcart Prize and short-listed for the Fish Publishing Historical Fiction Prize, among other honors. His essays have appeared in *Ninth Letter*, *Salt Hill*, *Swink*, and elsewhere, and been recognized as notable in Best American Essays 2009 and 2010.

The son of a Norwegian immigrant and a Texan, Stephan was born in Hanau, West Germany and raised between England and the United States. One of the last children of the Cold War, he graduated high school the year the Berlin Wall fell and studied screenwriting at USC Film School. After leaving Los Angeles, he worked as a cook, a video store clerk, a bartender, a driver of escorts, and finally a journalist, before returning to academia. The holder of a Master's degree in English Literature with a creative writing emphasis from the University of California, Davis and a Ph.D. in Literature and Creative Writing from the University of Southern California, he currently teaches at Augsburg College in Minneapolis.

While on a Fulbright Fellowship to Ukraine, Stephan lived in Kharkov, Ukraine's second-largest city, and traveled between Kolomyja and Volgograd, researching the mail-order bride industry. More recently, he lived in Belgorod, Russia, his wife's hometown.

Made in the USA
Lexington, KY
13 August 2012